90 Days of Pleasure

MARIE MCKENZIE
and
USA TODAY Bestselling Author
NALEIGHNA KAI

Marie L. McKenzie, LLC
Orlando, Florida

90 Days of Pleasure

MARIE MCKENZIE

and

USA TODAY Bestselling Author

NALEIGHNA KAI

♦ ACKNOWLEDGEMENTS ♦

Marie McKenzie

First, glory and honor to my Lord and Savior. Special thanks to my husband, George, for your love and support throughout this journey, and for allowing me the creative space I need. I love you lots.

Special thanks to Naleighna Kai, book whisperer, my co-author, writing coach and editor. Without you I may not have discovered this craft. I love and appreciate you more than I am able to express with words.

J.L. Woodson your covers inspire me to open the books they grace.

J.L. Campbell, my friend, mentor, and book coach for the encouragement and uplifting words when my days are not unfolding the way I want them.

To NK Tribe Called Success, my phenomenal community for having my back always and keeping me covered.

To those who constantly support, encourage, and keep me straight: the Neitas, the Briscoes, Aunt Herma, brother O'keile, family and friends—too many to name here.

Those I didn't mention by name—family and friends—and may have forgotten, thank you for all the love and cheers. May God continue to lift you higher and use you for His glory.

To the author groups, book clubs and readers who have purchased and read my book, your support means a lot.

Naleighna Kai

Special thanks goes out to: The Creator from whom all Blessings and opportunities flow, Sesvalah, my son, J. L. Woodson (for the awesome cover designs for the Pleasure Series), Sesvalah, Janice M. Allen, Debra J. Mitchell, Royce Slade Morton, Bunny Ervin, J. L. Campbell, Kelly Peterson, Janine A. Ingram, Ehryck F. Gilmore, LaVerne Thompson, Kassanna Dwight, Betty Clawson, Amanda McCoy, Brynn Weimer, the Kings of the Castle Ambassadors, Members of Naleighna Kai's Literary Cafe, the members of NK Tribe Called Success, the members of Namakir Tribe and Nakaeri Tribe, and to you, my dear readers . . . thank you all for your support.

Chapter 1

"They are going to kill you. We have to hide you on a commercial flight."

Crown Prince Amir tried to tamp down on his mounting anger—to no avail. He was en route home when his security team received word of trouble in Nadaum because of a minor misunderstanding of something he had done while visiting the country. A trivial thing, surely, that did not warrant the assassination plot on his life that had been uncovered. Someone wanted to take him out to send a message to his father, Sheikh Aayan of Durabia. His entourage, security, and advisors had immediately detoured the jet to Chicago to ensure his safety.

"Commercial?" Prince Amir asked, enraged at the inconvenience.

Without hesitation, his advisor, Kamal, replied, "That is the only way we have to ensure you get home in one piece."

"I am not concerned," he barked, dismissing them with a flourish of his jeweled hand. "I do not wish to fly with commoners. Nadaum wouldn't dare do something brash while they are in negotiations with my father."

He stomped to his feet, pushed the chair away from the table and marched to the edge of the room scanning the array of paintings and furnishings. "You expect me to sit on a plane with those people?" His eyes seemed to pierce through the members of his entourage.

The sign outside of the VIP lounge at Chicago O'Hare Airport read "Out of Service." Angry executives and other VIPs, too upper crust to mix with the public, milled about seeking alternate accommodations while they awaited their flights. However, thirty minutes prior, bystanders observed four well-dressed men flanked by several other men in dark suits being escorted through the entrance. The way they moved in tandem and the discreet earpieces, signaled that a covert operation was afoot to protect a visiting dignitary. Most who were already situated in the room, had been gracefully relocated to an opposite side but were none too happy about the new developments. Finally, the airport staff caught on to the ruse created by Amir's people and opened the Lounge again to First and Business Class customers.

Kamal's ringing phone halted the heated conversation taking place in the VIP Lounge.

"Your wife needs to speak with you now, sir." Nasir, one of the guards rushed to Prince Amir's side and handed him the cellphone.

He snatched it up, walked over to the far side of the room and stood with his back towards them. His pacing hinted to onlookers that the conversation was not going well. His people were well accustomed to the hellraising that was often dished out by the beautiful Faiza. After a few minutes of angry whispers he stomped, turned around, rolled his eyes, and yelled, "I know you just had a baby. I will be there as soon as I can!" He then slipped the phone in his pocket, glared at the people who dared to look his way as he walked back towards the guards.

"All right, I need to get home before she raises the palace roof. So, I will go along with your plans. I will fly among these … commoners, but only this time," he announced as he approached the group. "You will find this threat and neutralize it. Do not wait for my father and Sheikh Zoraib to work things out."

"What caused you to change your mind?" Kamal asked, knowing it could not be due to any concern for his wife and newborn child. More likely, it was due to the new women they had brought in to El Zalaam, a private club that provided an array of entertainment for men with … wicked and eclectic tastes.

His eyes blazed as he reported, "Faiza told me that my father is having private conversations with Kamran. I am Crown Prince and Kamran is no one, but his sudden popularity with my father is concerning. So, I have to get to the bottom of whatever has transpired. Faiza is even laughing at me, saying that Kamran may now be father's favorite in my absence." He paced from the door to across the room with four pairs of eyes fixed on his every move. "He changes favorite sons like he changes his undergarments."

Prince Amir, the offspring of one of the Sheikh's six wives from the elite families of Durabia, Nadaum, Jordan and United Arab Emirates—UAE, was currently next in line for the throne. His brother Salam, one of the oldest was one of Sheikh's favorite and someone to watch, but his brother, Kamran, had fallen out of favor a long while ago. Amir's ascension to Crown Prince was due to an unfortunate mistake in Kamran's generic footprint, but it appeared there might be some reversal of fortune in the making.

Kamran Ali Khan, once the Sheikh's favorite and heir apparent, had always been hated by his brothers, especially Amir, because of his lofty plans and visions for Durabia that pleased their father. Thankfully, a plot devised by the wives meant Kamran would forever remain an outcast. Or so he was until a few days ago. Somehow, the people of Durabia loved Kamran. Especially the women who fawned over him since it had been said he was the most handsome of all the princes.

"Now this nonsense about secret meetings," Amir snarled. "Get me home without delay."

"We will make it so, your highness."

The airport was already in chaos. Stranded passengers wandered aimlessly, most unable to speak with a human at the ticketing counters due to international unrest in the Middle East. Canceled and delayed flights had been the highlight of the day. Emirates, United, and Delta were mostly impacted and were working frantically to get their VIP passengers to any number of destinations.

"Durabian Airline, where may we fly you better today?" Nasir had the phone on speaker, and it was answered on the first ring.

"I am calling to confirm flight number EK 235 to Durabia."

"So sorry sir, that flight is delayed at this time," said a pleasant voice on the other end. "We might not be able to get you out of Chicago until tomorrow morning. We'll get back to you when we have an update."

Prince Amir flung a chair across the room, grabbed the phone from Nasir's hand and without breaking the connection, hurled it to join the chair.

"Get me out of here, now," he roared. "Why did you bring me here and now I cannot leave this horrible place? I cannot even venture outside because I will be surrounded by peasants." He paced and stomped around the room like a two-year-old, kicking any object within reach of his feet. As he came near to his entourage, he offered them a glare and they shrank back before he turned and punched the wall, yelled, and grabbed his right hand.

A towel with ice was quickly procured and thrust towards him, which he grabbed and wrapped around his visibly swollen hand.

Something or someone would ease his discomfort and fears that he was about to lose his position as the most powerful man in the Middle East. *Hmmmm. Preferably a woman.*

As he soothed his fingers, he gently flexed and extended them to check for normal function. Satisfied, he wrapped the towel around his hand and smiled through the pain.

Most definitely a woman.

Chapter 2

"How could you do that to me? I don't want to go," Alicia said, turning her focus on Dallas.

The conversation had been on replay for some time and Alicia's response was always the same. She was not prepared to bare her soul, not now, not ever. Her mind was made up, and she would not relent, no matter how much coaxing from Dallas. No matter how much he was right.

Alicia moaned and twisted out of his embrace. "I can't do it. I just can't."

Dallas remained calm, and breathed softly, probably as exasperated by the process as she was. "We'll do it together, sweetheart. You'll never have to go it alone—ever again."

She waved him off. "Not now, Dallas. Not now."

He loved her, as no other, and she knew it, but had a hard time accepting.

Am I worthy of such unguarded love and devotion?

Most of her life, she had been used and abused, so this almost being worshiped feeling, was totally foreign.

Alicia Mitchell wasn't afraid to dismiss those who propositioned her if she didn't find them up to her standards. To date, especially after Taric Hasan damn near killed her, no one seemed to measure up. She was not about to let anyone play fast and loose with her mind, body, and soul.

Dallas wants me!

Alicia found that almost impossible to digest.

She couldn't believe that one day she could be free from the pain and sadness, a result of

the evil that her family and troubled relationships had unleashed. How could she ever believe that what Dallas was showing her was real and could be sustainable? He could have any woman he wanted, there were many lying in wait. Some even blatantly throwing themselves at him wherever he went. Yet, he declared his love for her and that she was his only desire.

He moved past the bed and ottoman, walked over, and pulled her to his chest, then wrapped her in a tight embrace. "Yes, my love, we are going to do this. This time away can serve two purposes, pleasure and alleviating your pain."

Alicia buried her face in his neck. "I don't want to talk about it with anyone. I barely mentioned it to you." She softly pushed at his chest in an attempt to break free from his arms.

"This time will be different," he promised. "It's time for soul searching and healing on a deeper level." His left arm tightened around her, while he cupped her chin with his right hand and gazed into her eyes. Her efforts to step out of his hold were futile, not that she was fighting very hard, because being in his arms was her happy place, no matter what the circumstances.

They were standing in the middle of the master bedroom of an Executive Suite at the exclusive Peninsula Chicago Hotel. It was NBA offseason and Dallas had brought her for the weekend to wine and dine, prior to the big trip to Durabia he had just now dropped in her lap. He had already finalized the itinerary, although she had objected, with the hope that she would eventually come around to his way of thinking.

"Different? How?" She asked.

Alicia's gaze wandered through the open window to the skyline across the way. As the night lights flickered, her mind drifted to her life and what had brought them to this topic, again.

"The vibe in Durabia is unlike anywhere we have ever been. Just us enjoying each other and we'll consult the therapist in between." He cupped her chin and gazed into her eyes. "Let's schedule one consult and go from there. How does that sound, baby?"

Alicia gazed up at him and offered a hesitant smile, then added, "We'll see," before moving towards the window.

As their relationship grew, she became more comfortable with him, and had shared episodes of her traumatic past. When she opened up to him the first time, he was compassionate and caring, and his love and devotion remained unchanged. However, now he wanted to go further. Dallas wanted her to seek therapy for sexual violence and other unresolved harrowing experiences. He was patient, loving, and kind as he sought her approval in engaging her in the discussion of her past and how to get her the help she needed to overcome, survive, and thrive. She was no pushover. More strong-willed and sometimes refused help, even when the need was blatantly obvious.

"There's a special place in Durabia where survivors, just like you, are transforming their lives," Dallas explained as if the request was the most normal thing in the world.

"The thought of going to Durabia scares me," she exclaimed, while twisting in his arms, which he finally relaxed, and she stepped away and dropped down on the bed.

"What do you know about the place?" He asked, as he left the window, stood by her side, and rested one hand on her shoulder.

She looked up at his six-foot plus stature, pulled herself backwards and asked, "Isn't that one of the places in the Middle East where women, especially ones like me, are treated lower than tenth class citizens?" She fixed her gaze on him, as if to dare him to disagree.

"It won't be like that, my love." Dallas edged closer with open arms. "We'll be in the Free Zone where you would have all the freedoms possible, almost like being in America."

"Really? Like America? I find that hard to believe."

She had been thinking of a nice long vacation with Dallas in a romantic place somewhere her mind could roam free of anything related to her past or trauma. Something she kept attracting for some reason. The past eighty days proved that fact. They had enjoyed a few romantic getaways. She didn't want to deal with the itchy feel of the past gnawing at her skin and driving her towards insanity. She was already getting a mega dose of that just from this discussion with Dallas.

"I know you really wanted to go to India. This is the closest we can get for now. There's a special counselor there, who I believe will be the best person for you to speak with. She's American and well-known for her work there and in the States."

"I'll think about it." She walked over to the window, leaned on the edge, folded her arms before turning to face him.

"That's better than no," he responded with a smile.

She hesitated at first, then smiled sheepishly and rubbed her stomach. "I'm feeling famished after all this deep talk.

"Room service or you want to go out?" Dallas asked with raised eyebrows.

"I need some fresh air," Alicia answered as she grabbed a black purse from the dresser, stepped into a pair of tan sandals, and with a smile, headed towards the door. "Especially since you're trying to lock me up on a plane for thirteen hours."

Dallas returned the smile, grabbed the rental car keys and they took the elevator down to the Shanghai Terrace to dine on some sumptuous Asian cuisine. After an enjoyable couple of hours feasting on spicy crisp beef tenderloin and Peking duck accompanied by sauteed mushrooms, steamed rice and vegetables and enjoying each other's company, they returned to their suite.

Alicia stated that she wanted to get into something more comfortable and headed for the bathroom. Dallas quickly followed and asked, "Are you all right with me embracing you right now?"

"Of course." She faced him and wrapped her arms around his middle, placing her head on the wall of his chest.

"You don't need anything more comfortable. As a matter of fact, you don't need anything at all." He unzipped the back of her dress and slid it from her shoulders, letting it fall to her ankles, revealing her smooth creamy skin, adorned in red lacy Fenty bra and panties.

"Dallas, what are you doing?" She asked, in a breathy whisper, as he rained kisses across her neck and face.

"I'm loving you. Let me love you, Alicia." The erection pressing into her abdomen was evidence of his desire.

She moaned, feeling the warmth spread to her center. Her mouth was tempted to say no, but her body was yelling, "take me to the stars again."

No denying the tug-o-war going on inside her head. On their own accord, her arms slid upward around his neck, and she pressed her body into his. Evidently, he felt the heat and responded in kind. The rest of their clothes went flying as they rushed to satisfy the passion welling up inside.

He guided her to the bed, placed her on the edge, then he knelt on the floor and hoisted her legs on his shoulders. His head lowered and he played her like an expert tuner. Alicia's previous lovers were takers, so being pleasured was both foreign and enlightening.

'Dallas!" She looked down at the man who aroused more passion in her than any other, even the one with whom she had spent twenty-three years. Married at sixteen, her husband cared nothing about her pleasure. As a matter of fact, her pain was his pleasure—he made sure the experience was painful for her—because that was the only way he could sustain an erection.

Dallas moaned and continued as if dining on his favorite meal. "If I die right now, it's all right, because I'm in heaven." He lifted his head and smiled at her.

Alicia was unhappy with the brief separation and thrusted her hips forward to hasten the reunion. Her moans, coupled with the explosion of pleasure, was a testament of delight.

Dallas kept up the teasing and exploring and from the intense look in his dark brown eyes he was thrilled with her response. Soon shivers signaled that she was at the brink and release was near. He stopped, climbed onto the bed, and pulled her on top of the joystick. Alicia took control and did her absolute best to rock his entire world. It wasn't long before they were both holding tightly to one another, enjoying a sweet climax. They clung to each other as if letting go would somehow break a connection they never wanted to lose.

"Dallas, I trust you. We will go to Durabia as you planned."

He smiled down at her. Neither moved for some time, then she buried herself into him, he pulled her in, and they drifted off to sleep.

Chapter 3

Dallas was the first to open his eyes and he gave her a tight squeeze, which caused her to wake up.

"Good morning, beautiful," he said with a wide grin.

"Good morning to you too," she responded with a satisfied smile.

I could get used to this. She basked in the aftermath of the night's activities, as she snuggled closer. Not even a breeze could pass through them at this point. Alicia felt blessed, although her mind couldn't fully grasp that this kind of love, this kind of feeling, could last. Her mind kept playing back and forth games between the blissful feelings and the relationship that was unfolding between them.

Prior to meeting Dallas, she always seemed to attract the wrong kind of males. The ones who approached were often loaded with over inflated egos, lack of capacity to love or the ability to appreciate a woman of substance and acted as if they were God's gift to the female species. Her experiences so far had left her disillusioned, and with the thought that true love wasn't in the cards for her. She wouldn't dare to hope for love or even a strong show of affection from a member of the opposite sex who was worthy of her time.

Until now. Dallas Avery, NBA Superstar, a paragon of manhood with a heart of gold all wrapped into one. She felt Dallas' love seeping into her soul and wondered how she got to be so blessed. This was the first time she felt that a man cared about her well-being and wasn't sure how to receive it. On one level, she knew he loved her, but couldn't wrap her mind around it yet.

He pulled her close, "How about we decide on a date and secure a flight for Durabia?"

She knitted her brow and lowered her head.

"We can always cancel or postpone if you change your mind." He added while lifting her chin with one hand.

She nodded, placed her lips to his cheek and delivered a radiant smile.

This morning her heart was singing a happy tune but would it last? She gave Dallas a quick peck on the cheek, slid out of bed and headed to the shower. On the way, she twirled to give him a full display of her body. He smiled as their eyes locked, and she winked.

Dallas heard the water running, picked up the phone from the bedside table and ordered breakfast, which he expected to arrive at their suite before she left the bathroom.

Within minutes, there was a brisk knock on the door, and he ushered in a waiter dressed in a sparkling white uniform, rolling a brown-colored wooden food cart laden with bacon, eggs, fluffy pancakes, fresh fruits, and juices accompanied by coffee, tea, and sparkling water. The meal was served on all-white dinnerware and crystal-clear glasses, and he stowed the cart in the far corner of the living room near the door.

When Alicia joined him she was pleasantly surprised at the feast and sauntered over wide eyed and grinning.

"Are we having guests this morning?" She questioned with an eyebrow raised.

"No. Why?" Dallas asked, throwing his head back accompanied by a belly laugh, understanding her jest.

"Who's going to eat all that?" She waved her hand over the table.

"No worries," he responded, patting his gut, which caused her to erupt with laughter.

"I guess, everyone knows you can eat a cow and use a goat to wipe your mouth and still remain hungry," she teased.

"And that's not all I hunger for."

Alicia's cheeks flamed a bright pink color causing Dallas to give a low throaty chuckle.

     Marie L. McKenzie and Naleighna Kai

Chapter 4

The sun had just made an entrance into the Chicago sky. The ringing phone on the wall near the wooden hospitality desk had Prince Amir's advisor, Kamal, jumping to answer. He picked it up and heard, "Sir, your flight will be ready for boarding in thirty minutes."

He rushed past the broken chair and cellphone in the corner towards the prince, who was sitting in the lounge chair with his feet propped on the glass coffee table. He relayed the information and took a deep breath waiting for the verbal vitriol that would come.

"It is about damn time and I hope we have some pleasant food," he shot back, then stood, threw the towel and ice to the floor, and headed towards a concealed exit.

"Sir, wait," Nasir yelled as two members of the entourage rushed in front of the prince and edged him in.

"Wait for what? Let us get the hell up out of here before I lose my damn kingdom."

Kamran was only part of the rush. He also wanted to visit El Zalaam to have his first choice of the new girls being prepared and awaiting his return. His brothers had also been alerted to the fresh crop of flesh. The tender ones had been trained to do things his wife would never consider. How he managed to get Faiza with child was anyone's guess. She barely let him sneeze on her let alone sink between her creamy thighs.

Amir boarded first class flanked by his three aides. The members of the party appeared agitated as they took their seats and spoke in hushed tones. The other first-class passengers appeared uneasy as they noticed them huddled together. However, as the flight attendant started the safety proceedings all eyes became focused in her direction.

As he tried to fit in the unusual setting of a public plane, he watched each passenger as they entered, paying special attention to his fellow first-class mates. He was about to close his eyes for a much-needed rest when his heart hit pause. He sat up straight, blinked, and swallowed hard, as sweat peppered his forehead. Nasir, the guard on his right, jumped to attention, asking, "Are you all right?"

"Yes, I am," he replied, gazing at the woman who now occupied the seat one row across and in front of him. He cast a hostile stare at the over six-foot athlete-type escort with his arm draped around her in a show of possession obvious to any man who took an interest.

"Who is that?" he whispered, but it was loud enough for the rest of his party to hear.

Nasir and the two other guards laughed with unease as they watched him, because they were too familiar with his lust for women other than his wife, but had never shown an interest in an American woman, as he was doing now.

"She is exquisite," he said, boldly continuing his appraisal. "I want her."

"We will find out who she is," two of them replied in unison, as they were commanded by Sheikh Aayan to always grant his son's wishes. What Prince Amir wanted, he would be provided, no matter the circumstances or consequences. And most times the consequences were dire. They had narrowly escaped from Nadaum and hid out in neighboring Jalanar, allowing a little time for things to settle.

Now he was sitting in first class, heart pounding, as he laid eyes on a woman who caused his qadib to throb and swell while fighting for an exit out of his undergarments.

Prince Amir winked at the leggy Asian flight attendant whose knee-length brown skirt and long matching jacket caressed her assets as she sauntered up and down the aisle. The Raspberry red hat on top of the French twist complemented her enhanced red lips and bright smile. He beckoned her with his right index finger and her eyes took on an exited brilliance as she practically skipped to reach him.

He whispered, "I have an important request."

She leaned in closer to get the details.

"Please remove *everyone* from first class except my people and my new friends over there." He directed his gaze towards the woman with creamy skin, dark silky hair, green eyes that glittered like jewels sitting with the man with an air of importance that matched Amir's vibe. He held out his right hand to Nasir who slid in some currency. Her eyes flashed and smile widened as the wad of American dollars told the story. He thrust the money into her palm and watched as she straightened her back, slightly disappointed as she strutted away and briskly entered the cockpit. The couple across from him were so engrossed in each other, they were oblivious to the fact they were the object of much nefarious thoughts and possibly unwanted attention.

A satisfied smile played across Prince Amir's face as he leaned back in his seat and closed his eyes, savoring the mental imagery of what would happen. He felt the heat of his team's gaze, opened his eyes again and said, "wait for it. Just a small change of plans."

The entourage shared curious glances as Nasir's eyebrows snapped up, then nervous laughter filled their compartment. The woman he had his eye on was definitely not his normal fare. American, and for all appearances a bit older than the man who was looking at her with such adoration, everyone could feel the love from across the aisle.

Nonetheless, she was amazingly beautiful. Regal even.

"Ladies and gentlemen in first class, we have some issues and will be asking some of you to deplane at this time."

Armed with the knowledge that the handsome Middle Eastern was in fact, Crown Prince Amir of Durabia, the petite beauty, joined by other members of the cabin crew, wandered throughout the cabin whispering to visibly upset passengers. Exorbitant airline vouchers, a hotel stay at a five-star Chicago hotel of their choice, and plenty of cash were quickly and discreetly exchanged, which turned frowns upside down and caused occupants to rapidly gather their belongings and move towards the exit. Another group of men came in and spread out in the first-class seats and began chatting with Amir's team.

As Dallas stood and placed his right arm around Alicia's shoulder to assist her into the aisle and make an exit, Amir nudged Kamal who sprang into action. No one had approached them with incentives, so they didn't expect them to leave.

"You are to remain in first class," Kamal commanded.

Dallas shot him a dagger stare which caused him to step backwards to put ample space between them.

"He means, as our guests," Nasir added smoothly.

Dallas eyed both of them for a moment, then gently tugged at Alicia's arm to hasten their departure.

Amir glared at the Asian flight attendant, tapped his palm, and raised an eyebrow.

She rushed up the aisle. "Mr. Avery and Ms. Mitchell you're required to remain aboard because ..."

This time Alicia's shoulders tensed.

"We can't retrieve your luggage and we won't be able to reunite you with them," the attendant announced as she approached and extended her arm to place a hand on his shoulder.

A stoned-faced Dallas shrugged, stepped backwards, causing her outstretched arm to land by her side as he pulled Alicia towards his chest.

Dallas kept his focus on the flight attendant. "So, you're somehow able to find *everyone else's* luggage but not ours?"

"I … I … I do apologize for the inconvenience. Everything will be all right."

"Dallas, please …"

"Yes, listen to the sensible woman," Amir taunted, putting his focus on Dallas. "So we can leave this godforsaken place. Do not worry. I will compensate you fully for your troubles."

"I don't need your money," Dallas shot back as Amir gave a dismissive wave to the flight attendant who whirled around and went to whisper something to her co-workers who instantly went in different directions.

He turned to look at the five men sitting across and behind him, then at the new men who had come aboard, turned faced her head on and said, "All right? That's questionable."

Amir moved his index finger in a circle and two of the attendants sprang towards the cabin doors.

"We are getting off of this plane right now," Dallas said, his hand on the small of Alicia's back.

The door agent announced end of boarding. The plane door slammed shut and the flight attendants flipped the lock.

"Dallas, don't make a scene," Alicia said, stroking his arm.

"There's nothing in those suitcases that we can't replace," he said with a pointed look at the other First-Class passengers who had their focus on them.

"Those pictures of my niece?" she countered as the plane pulled away from the gate without waiting for Dallas, Alicia, or the flight crew to take their seats. "The one I mentioned was like a daughter to me? The last ones that I have of her? I meant to put them in my tote but forgot to pull them out."

Dallas' shoulders lowered with defeat. He guided her back to the seat and buckled in as the plane taxied towards the runway.

Chapter 5

Crown Prince Amir's ruse to empty the first-class compartment of the other passengers and put more of his men in place had worked. He was brought up with the knowledge that there was little that status and money couldn't accomplish where he and his family were concerned.

His request for the identity of the two remaining passengers proved enlightening. The information handed to him by the flight attendant and what his team was able to ascertain, revealed a stunning Alicia Mitchell gazing up at a smiling Dallas Avery, evidence of the latest paparazzi assault that had been squelched for media purposes, but still existed on the dark web. Amir knew all about those things even though his father would never approve. Whenever his father's reign ended, Amir had every intention of instilling Sharia Law down to the letter. He would never have to go through the amount of effort that transpired over the past half hour to have a woman he wanted. His power would be absolute. Alicia Mitchell would learn that firsthand. Dallas Avery too, with that confidence he wore as if a man of his ilk deserved the finer things in life. He could do with one less valuable thing in his life. His woman would do nicely.

"Are you satisfied, Prince Amir?"

"Not until I have her in my bed," he shot back. "You see the way she looks at him?"

Nasir nodded.

"I want that. I want her to give me that kind of affection."

"She loves him," Nasir countered with a resigned sigh. "You cannot force a woman to love you."

"Can I not?" Amir shot back glaring at him. "I will take something close to it. She will definitely learn."

Nasir watched the couple for several minutes. "Prince Amir, I ask that you reconsider. She is clearly in love with that man."

"Do you think I care about that?" he snarled, gripping the arm rest. "If I thought he would not create a scene that would warrant the pilots turning this plane around and back to Chicago, I would take her right now."

"That would not be wise," Kamal said.

"You think I do not know that?" Amir snapped. "When we arrive in Durabia, then they will be in my purview. We will take her then."

"Sir, you do realize he is a celebrity. A *sports* celebrity. Americans love the athletes. This will cause an international incident. We are trying to keep peaceful relations with the United States."

"Well, they are not going to cause a stir for one woman. They will be in *our* country, *our* rule. Trust me. She. Is. Mine."

Nasir inhaled and let it out slowly.

"They will be staying at the exclusive and private Jumillah Hotel on the island," the prince announced, while flipping through the electronic tablet in his hand. "Find a way to get her away from him and bring her to me. That should not be hard. I do not think they know anyone in our country."

Nasir looked from one guard to the other and replied, "We will make some calls so our people can be in place and intercept them before they even check in."

Excitement and a little panic registered on the faces of the men.

"I am going to finally have a taste of an American Woman," he whispered, barely holding back an excited laugh as he glanced at the faces of his men.

"We are going to pull off a James Bond," Nasir said, a wide grin on his lips and his gaze roamed the faces of the men around him who were warming to the idea. "We will see to it sir." His eyes then leveled on the prince who nodded his approval and flashed a gaze at Alicia Mitchell and smiled.

"The moment we have communication available, make sure a private residence is prepared near the palace. Once I put the issues with Kamran to rest, I do not wish to be disturbed."

"Sir ..."

"If she pleases me, then I will install her in a private chamber in the main palace or a residence in the Free Zone."

"What happens if she proves difficult and will not acquiesce?" Nasir asked. "You know American women are given freedoms that our women will never know."

"That is unfortunate ... for her. I will personally break her and enjoy every moment."

"And if you cannot? You will return her to her American mate?"

"No ..." he replied with a growl. "I will kill her."

Chapter 6

"Let's try to relax and enjoy the flight as much as possible," Dallas said as he flipped through an eye-catching brochure, still trying to get his temper under control. "They are surely rolling out the red carpet in first class."

Alicia's heart pounded in her chest as she sat beside Dallas. She raised an eyebrow and quickly glanced at the smiling stewardess walking by their row. "It's very hard to be at ease seeing we were practically forced to remain on the flight."

After the atmosphere in the plane calmed, the captain stopped by first class and reassured the guests that everything would be fine, and they would arrive at their destination safely. Something still seemed "off."

The luxury of flying first class had temporarily wiped away the negative thoughts of Durabia from her mind during the flight. The pure comfort and elegance of the accommodations left her invigorated after the thirteen-hour flight. It offered superior upscale seats that completely reclined into a comfortable bed with snugly bedding, personal television and entertainment system, personal mini bar, made-to-order food service throughout the flight, an indulgence kit, which included a special made skincare collection, not to mention the spa bathroom.

Dallas and Alicia eventually settled in and went all-out on the flight, partaking of the appetizers, entrée—beef wellington with steamed vegetables—desserts and snacks. Although the cocktail list was extensive they settled for a classic champagne cocktail. Sleep was blissful.

When the large seat reclined, it provided ample space for a bed and after the door was closed, the suite transformed into a private domain.

* * *

As the flight neared Durabia, Alicia opened her eyes and peered through the window at the bright sunlight peeking through the clouds thousands of feet up. She stretched and looked over at Dallas, who still had his eyes closed and was breathing steady. She patted his arm, and he opened his eyes and smiled at her. "Join me in the spa," she urged, and he shook his head.

"If I go in there with you, we'll be in there for the rest of the flight."

Well, that was the whole point, right?

Two hours before the flight landed, Alicia, took advantage of the inflight Spa and the collection of toiletries alone. She was amazed at the spaciousness of the bathroom and amused when she returned to her seat to find fresh fruits and tea that the crew had left to complement her bath.

As she left the spa, her eyes flashed around her surroundings and clashed with the intense stare of the prince in a white dishdasha and tan iqal. His gaze sent shivers of uneasiness up her spine because it was filled with unbridled lust, reflective of Gerald Weens who had that same nefarious intent in Scotland. Then again with Taric Hasan in Texas. She barely made it out of those experiences alive. She quickly lowered her gaze and hastily returned to the seat. Dallas stirred and placed his arm about her waist.

* * *

As they exited the airline Terminal she was pleasantly surprised at the beauty of the airport and its surrounding areas. They strolled hand in hand through the massive crowd, passed shops and restaurants and array of local souvenirs in a last bid to have people take a slice of Durabia home with them to wherever they traveled in the world. Alicia gazed in wonder at the large indoor garden with lush trees, a large fishpond and was tempted to sit on one of the benches that lined its grounds and listen to the children gleefully playing in a special area, while their parents watch them intently. The tiled floors sparkled, although overrun with feet, as if the cleaning crew had been on a perpetual mopping spree.

Alicia's steps faltered as the hair stood on the back of her neck. She sensed that she was being watched and willed herself to not look around. She had a feeling that man was the type who still couldn't take a hint. Unable to restrain herself, she glanced over to her right and that familiar pair of eyes clashed with hers. He stared back at her, his desire palpable and unwanted.

"Dear God, please keep us safe," Alicia, whispered softly as they left the far end of the terminal. She gripped Dallas' hand for reassurance as her gaze wandered over the sea of faces bustling by—some to baggage claim, some to get on flights, while others were just there for the hellos and goodbyes.

"Miss Mitchell." The mention of her name caused her to miss a step. She knew who it was before she turned. She swung her neck to identify the speaker. Her mouth opened, but no words came, she grabbed Dallas' hand when she saw the same man, smiling at her.

As she tightened her grip Dallas turned and pulled her close to his body and faced the unwelcome stranger and the surrounding men as he said, "may I help you?"

The man stretched his right hand towards Dallas, but his eyes journeyed over Alicia from head to toe in an obvious lustful appraisal.

"I am Crown Prince, Amir, welcome to Durabia."

Dallas scowled and ignored the hand. "Thank you." He turned with Alicia and continued walking in the opposite direction as though they were being chased by the Devil himself.

"We are getting the hell up out of here," Dallas said, determination in his step. He whipped out his phone and made a quick call and followed with a text.

"Dallas, what are you doing?"

"We are taking the next flight home."

"What? No," she protested. "That was thirteen hours. No way in hell am I getting back on another flight without laying my head on a real bed, taking a real bath, and having a real meal."

"Alicia, I promised to keep you safe."

"We will be safe," she countered. "As soon as that prince is back in his palace he will forget all about us."

Dallas wasn't so sure. "Baby, we don't have to go home, but we need to get the hell up out of here. London, somewhere. *Anywhere* but here."

She hesitated a slight moment before saying, "all right."

With long determined strides and with Alicia nestled at his side, Dallas marched across the terminal over to the ticketing counter. "We need a flight out of here right now, please."

The raven haired ticketing agent raised one eyebrow and stared at him, "Sir, we have had a lot of cancelled flights today and everything else is booked."

Undeterred, Dallas pulled out his wallet and extended cash and credit card towards her, "I'll pay extra, anything. For anyone who is bumped off the flight. We need to leave tonight, right now."

She glanced at the screen, then to someone who came over to whisper something quickly in her ear causing her to stiffen, shook her head and replied, "No available flights. Not a single one. Folks have been waiting for hours, they want to go home."

Dallas peered at the second agent, lowered his head, forehead pinched tight as he pulled Alicia into a firm embrace and walked away from the counter.

Chapter 7

Alicia put a tight grip on his hand as they journeyed back the way they came, aiming to connect with the driver. She felt out of sorts as once again it seems she had attracted the wrong kind of attention through no fault of her own. Why did she keep having this same lesson time after time?

She had been passed from family member to family member who thought she was easy prey but didn't realize that her brother had taught her the use of a knife. She did have to use it at one point and the police hadn't questioned her too long since the man was half naked and in her bedroom when the ambulance arrived. No one had thought to drag him to the living room to match the lie they tried to tell.

Yes, life had cheated her of innocence, and way to soon. In addition, she married at an incredibly young age, and had endured a twenty-three-year union to a predator who was devoid of love and passion, accepting it as her lot in life. The only good thing she accomplished from that sham of a partnership, was financial freedom. He, a wily schemer, and she a savvy investor, who invested the proceeds from his insurance when he died, and the reward was a perpetual nest egg and the ability to live life on her own terms.

She nodded at Dallas while observing the crowd and was relieved that she had dressed appropriately. She had done some research online to find out what women were wearing in Durabia, making sure to follow the local norms and not attract unwanted attention. She was dressed in traditional Durabian attire, and although quite fashionable, it was still too conservative for her taste. Dallas had been incredibly pleased when she stepped out of the spa on the plane, fully covered and declared, "I'm ready."

Now those men in first class couldn't lay eyes on nary a curve.

Since they were travelling in August, and it was a little on the warm side, she had chosen a soft light tan-colored tunic with matching head covering. Not that Alicia Mitchell could avoid attracting attention. No Matter what she wore it always caused a head turn. Yes, she was beautiful and attractive, but she didn't always see or embrace it.

"Relax, my love," he whispered, resigned to staying only one night and then take the first thing smoking with wings or four legs—camels if need be. "You'll be fine, I promise." He squeezed her hand as they reached baggage claim and headed towards the expansive carousel swirling around with luggage of all colors, shape, and sizes ready for delivery.

"I can't help but worry. I have heard too many stories of women being mistreated in this hell hole called the Middle East, and we're here now. Also, that Prince gives me the creeps." She shook her body to show her nervousness.

Dallas lowered his lips to the top of her head, "You're safe with me my love."

They left the airport and stood outside the terminal looking for a sign that read, "DALLAS" so they could easily identify the driver. They didn't have to wait long. Within less than ten minutes a black SUV drove up and a smiling man with olive skin, wearing a white dishdasha and brown sandals, jumped out.

"Hello, I'm Zahri," he said, extending a hand. "You must be Mr. Avery and Ms. Mitchell."

"We are," Dallas responded, as he shook hands with the man and noticed that he didn't make the same gesture to Alicia.

"Luna received your message and sent me to escort you to her home," the voice laced with an Arabian accent conveyed. He picked up a piece of luggage in each hand, turned and walked towards the SUV, with its doors already open.

"What message?" Alicia asked.

"We'll talk later," Dallas responded as he grabbed her brown carryon bag from the curb.

They followed behind with Dallas slowing his strides ensuring that Alicia remained close to him. After their luggage was stowed, they entered and sat in the middle row and fastened their seat belts, Dallas leaned forward and whispered to Zahri.

Zahri glanced around, the vehicle roared to life, he stepped on the gas and hit the road navigating around throngs of other vehicles.

"Luna is looking forward to your arrival," he announced, as he turned the corner too deeply, corrected quickly, when the car ahead swerved dangerously into their path.

"We're excited to meet her also," Dallas replied, while he steadied Alicia with one arm and squeezed her shoulders.

"We have to get out of here fast," announced Zahri as he glanced in the rearview mirrors, then ahead. "We are being followed."

Dallas and Alicia hung onto each other and the seats in front of them. She frantically searched, seeing two suspicious vehicles gaining on them, causing her heart to race. Their bodies

bouncing on and off each other as Zahri drove at high speeds, zipped around street corners, and came close to crashing into several vehicles.

Zahri sped down the highway past a line of slow-moving vehicles.

"Pull over," the driver, an angry looking Arabian, shouted through the opened driver's window. "You cannot out drive us." The Arabian man pointed to the black SUV following closely behind.

Fear gripped Alicia as a blue SUV speeding on their right tried to cut them off, almost side swiping them.

"How did they spot us so quickly?" Zahri said as he twisted the steering wheel to avoid colliding into the car to their left. "Hang on, guys, and alert Luna."

The air filled with honking horns, screeching tires, and crushing metal as Alicia shuddered, glancing at the mangled vehicles they'd left behind. Her mind went on rewind of the images of her ordeals and wondered how they were going to get out of this situation alive. They were in a strange land and she had the feeling that that prince was behind all this. As if he sensed her apprehension, Dallas' forehead tightened and with eyes closed, he lowered his lips to the top of her head and banged his teeth as her head bobbed from the rough and bumpy ride. Dallas dialed Luna's number and relayed the information to her voicemail.

The black SUV ramped into their rear end, jarring their bodies forward. Zahri floored the gas pedal and the vehicle seemed to shoot through the highway like a bullet train. He zigged and zagged into a tunnel while glancing around frantically to spot pursuit. After a few minutes he declared, "I believe we have lost them."

Alicia exhaled and glared at Dallas. "Been here less than twenty minutes and narrowly escaped death."

Chapter 8

Their delayed trip ended at the luxury thirty-two story, Yaban Balk Residence building in the heart of Durabia's Free Zone. As the SUV approached, the tall black elegantly crafted metal gates swung open and Zahri rolled in, veered left into a massive garage and parked next to the three other luxury vehicles. They dashed out of the vehicle and entered the brightly lit space with grey tiled floors and were led to an elevator by a young fresh-faced smiling bellhop.

The glass panels offered unobstructed views of the massive first floor lobby furnished with exquisite blue and gold seating, long royal blue drapes with hints of gold, and floors covered with marble tiles in a honeycomb mosaic pattern. The elevator stopped on the twenty-eighth floor, and they stepped out into an expansive lobby and briskly walked past tall blue and gold flowerpots, which hosted live white and red plumeria, to a condo that rivaled anything she'd seen in Architectural Digest magazine. Not that they noticed much of its beauty.

As the door opened, a medium height woman with concern written all over her face, wearing a light green flowing tunic stepped towards them with outstretched hands. "I'm Luna Evangelista. Welcome to Durabia." She said hurriedly and ushered them into the condo. Inside she opened her arms for a hug, and they stepped in and embraced her as if she was a long-lost relative. Her friendliness and calm demeanor eased Alicia's discomforts about the therapy, but her mind kept drifting to the man at the airport and the chase to get here.

They stepped into the condo and Alicia's mouth formed an "O" as her gaze swept across the space. *She must have a thriving business because this place is breath-taking.* The furnishings from entrance to balcony were elegant, but not ostentatious. No expense was spared to make this a wellness retreat.

"Thank you for having us," Dallas replied, giving her a onceover before quickly pulling his focus on Alicia.

Luna looked from Dallas to Alicia and back, then with her gaze fixed on him asked, "So what happened on the flight from Chicago and here that had you so concerned? Your message was a little disturbing."

He stepped back, turned towards Alicia and relayed, "Crown Prince Amir was on our flight and I didn't like the way he kept eyeing Alicia. As we left the terminal he came over and introduced himself but kept staring at her as though he wanted her for himself."

Alicia nodded, her eyes fastened on Luna. "That man just makes my skin crawl."

"Sorry, my love. He got my blood boiling and that's not all." He dragged his hands down his face. "Zahri damn near drove at secret service speeds to get us here because several cars were chasing us. That's why we're here instead of our hotel."

The conversation halted due to a sharp knock on the door. Luna looked from Alicia to Dallas and knitted her brow. "I'm not expecting anyone else." She stood, placed her glass of orange juice on the side table, quickly walked to the door, peered through the peephole, and raised her right hand to her left breast as her heart rate picked up a frantic pace.

"Miss Evangelista, we need to speak with you urgently," a voice from beyond the door announced.

She slid back the bolt, turned the lock, and opened the door to three armed men dressed in Durabian military uniform. She stepped back and off to the side as they entered, eagle-eyed gazes sweeping the condo.

The stockiest member of the group said, "We are here to help."

"With what? I haven't reported a crime or asked for assistance," she responded, looking from one to the other before focusing on Alicia and Dallas who both tensed up with the unexpected visit.

"Crown Prince Amir has been asking a lot of unsettling questions about your guests." The short one turned toward the dining room; his eyes fixed on Alicia.

Damn.

Luna thought of the last minute careful plans she had made to ensure their safety. What had gone wrong? What did anyone outside of her circle know about what went on at her place?

"You have to leave now for your safety," the slender dark-haired officer pointed at Luna, before walking toward the dining room where Dallas and Alicia were observing.

She approached them. "I'm sorry." She glanced directly at Dallas. "Your fears were justified." Then turned to Alicia. "You've attracted some interesting attention from people higher up in the royal family and must be moved to a safe place, now."

Five pairs of eyes locked on her face as she spoke.

"Miss Evangelista, you have no need to worry," the tallest of the officers advised as he observed her moving closer to Alicia and softly patted her arm.

* * *

Alicia looked towards Dallas. She pulled her brows together and held onto his arm. Panic raced through her as she thought of what she may have done to bring on more events to threaten her safety. She recalled the other times when she was kidnapped and abused. *When will it end? When will men take no for an answer?*

"Miss Mitchell," the short officer addressed Alicia, "We will give you all the details later, but we must go to the place now."

Alicia looked from the officer to Dallas and then Luna as she realized that he would not be leaving with her. She didn't want to go without him.

"How do we know that these men are legit?" Dallas questioned, glaring at the men. "They could be collaborating with the prince."

"I know these officers personally," Luna said, gesturing to the trio. "We work together to protect the women at the shelter."

"I'm sorry baby," she told him as she clung to him, buried her face in his chest and his lips lowered to the top of her head.

She tried to step out of his hold, but he held on tight. Alicia looked up at him and then towards her untouched luggage which someone had fetched and placed by the door. She glanced behind her and noticed that the three officers were heading towards the front door, frequently glancing backwards to see if she was following. Alicia turned towards Luna, closed the distance between them and embraced her again.

"You'll be all right Alicia," Luna reassured her.

"Then why do I feel terrified? And why am I going to this place without the man I love?" Her gaze returned to Dallas and when she locked eyes with him, she saw anger and frustration wrapped together.

"They are taking you to the women's safety shelter and men are not allowed there."

Alicia released Luna's hand and headed towards the exit, two officers in front and one behind her, luggage in tow.

"You all had better stop right there," Dallas shouted as they neared the door. "Alicia isn't leaving here without me." He quickly closed the distance with long strides. He reached for her and pulled her to his side, as the officers and Luna both started speaking at once. He directed a laser stare at them, "I don't even care what you all have to say. She is N-O-T leaving without me. Got it?"

He walked back towards the living room with Alicia in tow and all eyes followed them.

Chapter 9

"Where is my father?" Prince Amir roared as he stormed through the palace doors trying to keep up with his entourage's stride.

Faiza left her seat beside the other women in the massive salon outside of the throne room and cast him a hostile stare. "Greetings to you too," she snapped. "You have not seen me in how many days, and you rush past me asking for your father?" She stretched out her hand to slow his movements as he continued, unmoved.

"I will get back to you," he snapped pushing her arm aside. "Right now, I need to know what's going on with my father and Kamran." He hastened his steps leaving her behind, nearly sprinting through the hallway towards his father's office.

With eyelids pulled down and lips tightened in a thin, disapproving line, her stare tracked him until he was out of sight, then she stormed away in the opposite direction.

Crown Prince Amir, current heir apparent to the Durabian throne, was still stewing with anger at the delay of having to travel on a flight that wasn't nearly as comfortable as a private jet. However, he was throbbing with excitement in anticipation of a rendezvous with the exquisite Alicia Mitchell. Memories of her and what he planned brought on a smile as he banged the gold knocker on his father's office door.

His knock went unanswered, so he went in search of Faiza, who always had a pulse on the goings on in the Palace. He had no idea how she knew everything long before he did. She was ambitious in every way that counted. Except bed. As he walked through the palace, he glanced at all the rich and elaborate décor and shuddered at the thought of losing it all to Kamran or anyone else. The Durabian fortune was massive, and the Khan real estate holdings extend to London, Europe, the United States and several islands.

Prince Amir grew up a spoiled rotten entitled child with the mentality of a man who's had life handed to him and sad experiences swept away before he could voice any displeasure. As he sauntered through the palace, the buzzing of his cellphone halted his thoughts on the woman who was so beautiful it caused an ache in all the wrong places.

"Sir, something is wrong. We did not intercept them at the airport and they did not check in. I called other hotels and they are nowhere to be found," Nasir announced. "I am watching the receptionist at the Jumillah Hotel scan the guest list for the third time and he cannot find any placement for them."

The news caused the prince to reach down and touch his qadib that jumped to attention in anticipation of good news, now it nearly shrunk in disappointment, the longing of being buried inside the gorgeous American woman was now on pause indefinitely or permanently arrested. "Find them," he commanded as he turned the corner and bumped into Faiza. The contents of the glass in her hand sent red stains down the center of her beautiful white dress and his dishdasha.

She jumped backwards and pressed her one-inch glass heeled pumps into the floor and screamed, "Look where you are going, you …" and stomped back in the direction from which she came, vigorously shaking her head as she departed.

Amir patted the front of his clothing and quickly followed. "I was distracted by the call." He patted her arm, whirled her around and lowered his lips to kiss her cheek, realizing he had better show her some type of affection or he wouldn't get any of the information he needed.

She pushed his shoulder and stepped backwards, raised an eyebrow, and pursed her lips. "Don't touch me right now," she snapped. "You shouted at me when I asked you to come home and few minutes ago you were so concerned about your father instead of greeting me. Not now, Amir. Not. Now."

"Oh, my dear, you just had a baby," he conceded, with an embarrassing smile. "It is the hormones. You will feel better soon." He moved closer, draped his right arm about her shoulder. "How is the little one?" He pressed his body closer to her and she stiffened.

"Ask your mother, she has been looking after the baby because I have been so tired. I need to get some rest now," she responded, placed the glass on the nearby table, pulled aside the golden drapes and sauntered down the hallway.

Amir remained unusually calm because he needed her on his side as he gleaned for answers. He hastened his steps to catch up. His sense of entitlement has led him to plot and scheme against his brothers, at times with Faiza's help, in order to garner his father's favor and remain the chosen one at all times. Afterall, he had come to learn that scheming against each other was almost encouraged by their father who liked to keep them on their toes which resulted in constant changes of Crown Princes, but never Kamran. Until now. His days as Crown Prince may be numbered, but he's not willing to go down without a fight.

Someone wanted him dead and he couldn't understand why things had reached that level. Kamran was in secret meetings with their father, and he needed to be at the table during the peace meeting with the Nadaum officials to explain away his actions. But more importantly, he had a woman to find.

Chapter 10

The stocky officer shook his head, dropped the luggage by the door, walked past Luna into the living room. "Mr. Avery, her safety is top priority. They cannot get to her where she will be."

Dallas remained silent for a minute, then raised a brow and pulled Alicia closer. "I could hire a security detail while we're at the hotel. We don't want to put Luna in danger as well," he said as he guided Alicia to sit on the sofa and joined her. "We can leave and go anywhere. Luna actually has roots here and a lot of women to protect."

"Mr. Avery, you do not understand. They have people in every hotel who are loyal to them. Every single one." He turned towards Luna as he continued. "As she said, we have worked with her, and she knows us and the work we do to protect the women at the shelter."

Dallas focused on Luna and then back on the officers, stood, stuffed his hands into his pocket, walked past the group towards the window and gazed into the horizon. He lifted his hands, tossed them over his head and shook his head as if hoping to dislodge the answer to his current dilemma.

"I don't want to let her out of my sight," he responded as he made his way back to the sofa and sat with his hands on his knees. "I don't know you. I don't know if I can trust you. She is valuable to me. You don't know her. Yet, you're asking me to give her up without any reassurances at all."

"We will not do anything to risk her safety. The people we are dealing with have connections, but a few members of the Royal family are decent. Kamran Ali Khan is one of them."

"So, I'm supposed to just hand her over to you for safekeeping, right?" Dallas lowered his face into his hands and shook it vigorously and groaned, then turned and faced Alicia. "How do you feel about all of this my love?"

He thought of all she has been through and wondered when she would get some peace. His mind drifted to the conversations he had with Luna when scheduling the consultation. Bedsides her childhood traumatic events and horrific marriage at sixteen years old, she had been the victim of a kidnapping in Scotland and another in Dallas. He had started to think that the Devil himself has employed a legion to keep him and Alicia apart.

Dallas' heart skipped when he recalled the terror she faced in Scotland at the hands of the maniac who was an associate of her scheming deceased husband. A man who married her because of what he discovered about her ancestors and birthright, all unknown to Alicia. Then compounded it with the sociopath who almost caused her death a few weeks later.

I have to keep her safe.

"Mr. Avery, you cannot protect her here, but we can. Let us help," the short stocky officer chimed in.

The voice brought Dallas back to the present. "Tell me about the place where you'll be taking her."

The officer glanced at his colleagues, Luna and back to Dallas and Alicia. "I cannot say much due to the level of security. It's a secret location known only on an as needed basis. The women who are rescued from sexual and domestic violence and sex trafficking are housed there.

Security is so tight; it may need an act of God to penetrate." He faced Dallas and folded his arms across a barrel-shaped chest.

Luna went to the kitchen and came back with a tray laden with water, a bottle of Moscato, cheese, crackers and drinking glasses.

"I want to see the place you're taking her."

"Sir, the best offense is to make sure she is safe and that means you cannot go with us."

"I'm not feeling none of that." Dallas rubbed the back of his head as the exhaustion from the flight set in. He understood the secrecy behind the shelter but couldn't help thinking that it wasn't the place for his Alicia.

"What is Prince Amir and his family like?" Dallas asked, and then narrowed his gaze. "You know what? Never mind all that." He held up an index finger and gestured to the guards. "Just know this, I don't care about Durabia's connection with America. Politics. None of that. Let something happen to my woman and I'll burn this motherfucker down until there's nothing left but ashes and elbows. You hear me?"

Alicia blinked and did a double take.

Luna grimaced and lowered her gaze to the carpet.

The three guards tensed and shifted at those volatile words.

"Maybe we can make an exception and let him see the outside of the building," Luna added, as she shifted uncomfortably under the weight of his words.

Chapter 11

What is happening here? Kamran whispered as his eyes roamed the faces of the palace aides and guards, then landed on Amir. His gaze zoomed in on an iPad screen off to the corner in the hand of Amir's top advisor, Kamal. He advanced into the room, passed the group of men standing around Amir at the conference table, stopped beside Kamal and glanced at the screen. The picture on the screen caused one brow to raise and his lips to tighten. "Why are you …?" The screen went blank.

His mind raced to recall the names of the people in the picture or who it reminded him of. He shook his head to clear the fog, and quickly remembered.

"The American Basketball star and the woman the press is trying to lay their eyes on."

He frowned at the memory that a friend had told him that he had seen the couple at the airport in Durabia earlier that day. His gaze returned to Kamal and locked there as the man squirmed. Kamran's heartbeat quickened as he sensed that the group and the couple in the picture were somehow on a bad collision course.

Kamran's gaze narrowed as he took the visual journey around the room from face to face, noting the sheepish looks and lowered heads. *What are they planning?* His focus returned to Kamal before he turned and abruptly retraced his steps.

He stopped in the living room with its elaborate furnishings and decor, of gold, blues and purple, which signified royalty and luxury to the max. Standing close to one of the floor-to-ceiling gold drapes off to one corner he watched as the men filed out of the theatre one by one, looking from side to side, more suspicious by the minute.

Kamal was last to exit and spotted Kamran. He quickly looked away and attempted to pivot in the opposite direction.

That's troubling. What is he hiding?

Kamal stopped, stuffed his hands in his pocket, his shoulders lowered and turned. Now he looked more like a defeated foe than the mobster with sinister intention he appeared to be earlier.

"Greetings Kamal," Kamran said as he moved forward and extended his right index finger towards the theater.

Kamal's body stiffened and he shuffled back inside the theatre with Kamran immediately behind and pulled the door shut. "I-I d-o n-o-t know anything."

What is my brother up to that has his Advisor so nervous? It cannot be good.

"That is strange. I have not asked you anything." Kamran frowned, directing a finger at the iPad clutched under Kamal's right armpit. "Why were you looking at that particular picture?"

He gave Kamran a nervous look while shifting from one foot to the other. "Prince Amir wanted me to get some additional information."

Kamran raised an eyebrow and pulled his lower lip between his teeth. "What information?" he asked, moving closer to pluck the iPad from the man's wiry fingers. He opened the screen and the picture popped up. His eyes sought and found Kamal's. "Why?"

"He is obsessed with the American woman."

Kamran mulled over the meaning for a moment. "What did you say?"

Kamal sank into the nearest seat and lowered his head into his hands. "He wants us to bring her to him." He looked up at Kamran as the response took hold.

"Are you serious?" He lowered into the seat opposite Kamal. He knew Amir could be devious but had not imagined this extreme.

"He really wants her, sir. She is … exquisite. Exotic."

"Black," Kamran said. "He has been with American women before. The difference here is she is Black and belongs to a high profile Black man. That is the appeal. This would be an international incident. Yet another scandal Durabia should not be caught up in."

Kamran stood, shook his head, turned, and walked to the unlit fireplace, stopped, and stared at the beautiful floral decorations of reds, blues, white and greens on the mantle. He turned towards Kamal and saw fear in the man's eyes.

He retraced his steps to where Kamal was seated, when he added, "Do not let him know I told you, sir. He will kill me."

Kamran's lips clenched and his brows furrowed. He knew that Amir was selfish and would stop at nothing to get what he wanted no matter the consequences. *Self-absorbed!* Kamran looked at him noting the panic and realized Kamal was more right than he knew. Amir used his power to manipulate those around him. Sheikh Aayan spent more time unraveling the ugly threads woven by Amir's deceit, betrayals and misdeeds, that it was now costing lives instead of using that energy to rebuild the image of Durabia into a place that is the epicenter of the world. "I will not disclose that you told me. I want you to keep up your normal routine, but now report everything to me."

He nodded. "I will, sir."

"If you do as I ask, you will be safe." Kamran dragged his hands down the back of his head. He had to act on this information without involving his father or the Durabian authorities.

He was the only one who could take action, but the thought caused his heart to flutter. *Amir is not deterred by the bounty on his head in Nadaum.* Turning him over to face his fate is the only way to restore peace.

Chapter 12

I'm sitting right here.

Alicia sat quietly and listened as they spoke about, but not to her, feeling tired of others always taking away her choices. During her childhood, her deceased husband, all her life, and the decisions they made on her behalf were always to their advantage.

Life has never been easy for Alicia Mitchell. Thoughts of her troubled life caused her heart to beat out of rhythm—quiver— like she had been given a mega dose of caffeine. Abuse— sexual, physical, and verbal— of the worst kind, have been doled out throughout her childhood and into her adult years. From family members, especially the men, who thought they had a right to take what no child should be required to give. The list piled high, but each time she got knocked down Alicia always got up and stepped over what was thrown at her. She was a survivor.

Alicia had been intentionally working on herself—meditation, affirmations, travel, selfcare—daily, everything within her power to help her heal and become whole, or so she thought.

Alicia's thoughts panned to Dallas who was willing to love, cherish, protect, and guide her in the direction of total healing and hinder the evil that kept interrupting and threatening the peace and joy before she could grasp it. She was in Durabia for a time of fun, coupled with healing, which might never happen because once again, another man decided that he wanted to take what she wouldn't give even if he had asked. Dallas was her true love and wanted to provide her with a happy normal life. Deep inside, she was reaching for that joyful place with him despite her fears and doubts.

I'm tired.

She stood and all eyes turned in her direction as she walked past Dallas towards the food tray then helped herself to a glass of wine, some cheese and crackers then returned to her seat. She took a sip and put the glass on the coffee table.

"Dallas, I know you're doing what you believe is best for me and I love you for that." She lifted her glass and took another sip, then gazed over the rim. "But this time I'll choose."

Dallas moved to her side and rested one hand on her shoulder, tilted her chin and looked in her eyes, then looked at the others. "Sorry about all of this sweetheart. I'm angry about what you're going through and your safety is always my priority. What would you like to do?"

"From all the information we have, I can't stay here." She stood, glass in hand and faced her audience. "I was looking forward to spending private time at the hotel with you and enjoying Durabia, but from the look of things that's not safe either."

"What are you thinking? Where do you want to go?" Dallas asked.

"To the shelter," she replied, pointing her right index finger at the officers. "I'm thinking this vacation and therapy must take a back seat and safety should be the only focus right now." She kissed his right cheek, took a sip, and sat.

Dallas looked down at her from his six-foot plus height, loving her and aching for her at the same time. The panic that started when he saw the Crown Prince gazing at her intensified. That man and his cronies looked sinister and this whole affair is disturbing. They'd been working on the relationship and things were going well. This trip to Durabia was aimed at sealing the deal, but now what? Perhaps letting her go was the solution to having her for keeps.

"Great idea," the stocky officer said as he lifted a bottle of water and looked from Dallas to Alicia. "Miss Mitchell, your decision is the best right now." His gazed leveled in her direction. "We can re-evaluate the situation in a day or two."

"Yes," she mumbled as she took a sip from her glass and coughed.

"Good, we have a plan." He glanced at his colleagues, and they all looked at Luna, as he walked over and stood directly in front of her. "Only a selected few know this. Meet Agent Xeva, sharpshooter, sword thrower and martial arts expert, who will be with you twenty-four - seven while you are there. She has been a fixture at the shelter, so her presence won't be suspicious."

"What?" She asked as everyone seemed to be talking at once.

"Don't let the therapy handle fool you. She's lethal," he declared with a wink at Luna.

She recovered from the shock, to say, "Wow. Any more surprises for today?"

"No, we will set the plans in motion as soon as you are ready."

He walked over to his colleagues and Alicia moved closer to Dallas and wrapped her arms tightly around him. "Dallas," she breathed, "I love you with all my heart."

Chapter 13

So, this is what it's like to be in a shelter.

Alicia and Luna arrived at the women's shelter under the cover of darkness escorted by military personnel. The other women and staff gathered around to meet and welcome the newcomer. One of the women, dressed in a long fuchsia dress with matching head covering walked up, circled Alicia and in a smooth French accent said, "you're too well put together to be one of us." She looked from Alicia to Luna and back waiting for a response as if she dared them to deny what appeared obvious. "This woman is nicely dressed, not a hair out of place, no bruises, no tear stain on her cheeks and looks like she stepped off the cover of a magazine."

Luna gently touched her shoulder and faced the challenge. "Hi Lia, don't judge," and pulled Alicia closer to the woman, "Miss Mitchell belongs here because she needs our help and a safe place to stay."

"We are safe here for sure," she responded, turning, and walking towards the other women.

Luna reached and touched her arm and said, "How you came to be here may be different, but we all have a story." She thought of when Lia arrived under the cover of darkness after being rescued from a sex trafficking ring. The story she relayed was tragic. She was a French exchange student, studying at a university in the United States of America. One night she went out with friends and never returned to her sponsor's home. She relayed that she had accepted a drink from one of her class mates at a party and the next she remembered was waking up in El Zalaam being raped.

Lia lowered head, nodded and walked past the front rows of chairs towards the back of the room as cheers erupted from the other women.

Turning in the opposite direction, Luna signaled for Alicia to follow, passing by women, some sitting on sofas and others milling about chatting in the hallway. They arrived at one of the rooms with a closed door, she pulled out a key from her pocket and they entered a large suite, which boasts adjoining bedrooms with matching queen-sized beds, beige sofa, an ensuite and a mini kitchen. Luna watched Alicia enter the bathroom then return in a brown ankle-length dress and beige sandals.

"How about something to eat, Alicia?"

Alicia stopped beside one of the beds with Lilly-white sheets, then turned to face her. She was silent for a while. "Actually, I'm hungry. My last decent meal was on the flight." She wandered into the kitchen, opened the cupboard, and pulled out a blue drinking glass, added some apple juice, and pulled a stool from around the table and perched on the edge.

"Meals were prepared ahead of our arrival, so grab a plate and dive in." She opened the pots on the stovetop which contained jasmine rice and beans, miso salmon, steamed vegetables, and broccoli cheese soup. The aroma sent messages to the taste buds and stirred up the hunger pangs.

Alicia joined her by the stove, took a blue dinner plate, sampled the offerings, and returned to the table.

As the meal progressed Luna relayed how her life landed her in Durabia. "I loved my life in the military and when I retired, I chose to be a Sexual Assault Therapist and Self-Defense Coach, due to some of my personal experiences and those of people I knew. I also felt that I could teach the women the skills I acquired so they could defend themselves if the need arises. While chatting with a colleague in Chicago," she continued, "I had informed her that I needed to

change locations. I felt uneasy where I was, as if I wasn't fulfilling my purpose. Don't get me wrong, I loved the work I did there, and I provided value to my clients, but felt that there was something missing. She told me about the need for a Sexual Assault Therapist in Durabia and offered to connect me with someone she knew. I instantly felt a tingle and knew that this place was calling my name. Have you ever felt like God was sending you on a mission or calling you to serve? That's what I felt that night."

The following day her friend had called with information needed to launch an exploration into the possibility of relocating to Durabia, including contact information to the famous Suha & Suha Realtors, the finest in the city. As she spoke, Luna thought of the other reason she needed a change of scenery. The love of her life, Zach, had left on a trip around the world two years ago and had not been seen or heard of since, although he had promised to call, write and return for their wedding. She had fallen in love with him after his mother, one of her clients, had introduced them five years before he vanished.

"Amazingly, the realtors were available 24/7, so, although a nine-hour time difference existed I called and scheduled a tour of this beauty. It was love at first sight. It spelt wellness-retreat, and that was exactly what I needed for me and my clients. My work in Durabia and particularly at this shelter includes self-defense."

The shelter was tucked away in the Durabian Free Zone and spread out on four acres of land, with no other building in close proximity, and looked like high-end apartments to curious onlookers if they trespassed that far from the road. All staff were trained in self-defense and three military officers were discreetly stationed in and around the premises 24/7. Security was tight. Doors were kept locked, and the women are encouraged to not venture outdoors alone after dusk. Most importantly, besides the military guards, men are not allowed anywhere inside the building.

As she spoke, Alicia listened intently and was particularly interested in her tale of self-defense. Like Luna, although not professionally trained, she was a skilled knifewoman, complements of her brother, and also dabbled in martial arts. Thanks to Dallas, she owned a Glock 42, and wasn't afraid to use it. Especially given what happened in Scotland and Taric's reappearance in Dallas. She remembered when Dallas helped her to make the choice—one of the most popular handguns for women—light, sleek and reliable with a seven round capacity and uses .380 caliber ammo.

"How long do you think we'll need to hide out here?" Alicia asked, transferring dishes from the table to dishwasher, clearing the dining table and wiping the table with a dish rag.

"We're still assessing the situation, so it's hard to tell right now." She cocked an eyebrow, shook her head while draining the contents of the wine glass. "We're hoping by tomorrow we'll have some intel to get you all out of the country. Let's settle in and make the best of it. I'm frustrated that I'm not able to give you a definitive answer," Luna said, her gaze fixed on Alicia. "How do you feel about starting a conversation about your past? I believe working with you now will prepare you for the wonderful things coming in your future."

Alicia looked at her and smiled. "You know, I was thinking about that, especially since hearing a little about these women's stories, what they've been through and how much you've helped them." She left the dinner table, walked over to the sink and gazed through the window across the night sky.

Luna joined Alicia and held her hands. "Are you sure?"

"I'm very sure," Alicia replied, "I'm beginning to accept that Dallas was right, I really need this."

"That's the first step, accepting, and then opening up." Luna then guided Alicia out into the hallway past the group therapy room where some of the women were socializing. Two doors down, she opened a blue door that led into her private office, where she had all the necessary resources—manuals, affirmation and meditation guides—to help Alicia.

Careful thought went into making this space therapeutic for the women who entered. The décor and furnishing married peace and tranquility and they were in harmony. The soft neutral tones of beige on the walls were complemented by soft blue drapes, beige sofas and recliners with multicolored accent pillows. The most dramatic accent was the floor to ceiling magic fountain with a stream softly and peacefully cascading down the wall. The sound was like a lullaby.

Luna rushed to her side. "Alicia, are you all right?" she asked, placing a hand on her shoulder and steering her to the leather sofa and claimed the space beside her.

Alicia could only shake her head.

After a few minutes, she wiped her eyes, looked at Luna and said, "I'm ready to start my healing journey."

Luna stood, patted Alicia on the shoulder and walked over to her desk, retrieved a note pad, then returned. Luna recalled the answers to the questionnaire that she had completed with Alicia. She had garnered necessary background, social and medical information, everything she needed to formulate a unique therapy plan.

"I understand it may be difficult to talk about what happened to you," Luna said, as she locked gaze with Alicia.

"Before now, I wasn't looking forward to this," Alicia said, lowering her gaze to her hands that were resting on her lap.

Luna shifted in her seat and her eyes swept over Alicia, noting that her shoulders had tensed. "What inspired the change tonight?"

"I walked in and saw all those women whose stories were similar to my own, some far worse. They are here getting the help they need. That drove the point home that I'm not alone. If they can receive healing, so can I." She stood, walked past the desk and coffee table over to the window to gaze across the horizon. Then she picked up a bottle of water from the silver food tray in the corner by the window and drank half before returning to the place she had just vacated.

Alicia slowly shook her head and looked at Luna, "I look at those women out there and see the radiance on some of their faces and felt in my heart that despite what they have been through, they are survivors, and I want that. I want that for me."

"You can have that," Luna said gently patting Alicia's hands. "You deserve that. We're going to work together to get you to the place where Alicia Mitchell is whole."

Alicia nodded, took deep breaths in an effort to calm herself.

Luna moved closer. "How are you feeling right now?"

"It's getting hard to breathe," Alicia said, as her breath came in shallow bursts.

Luna knelt beside her and squeezed her hands. "Do you remember those exercises we discussed?"

"Yes," Alicia said, closing her eyes and inhaling slowly and releasing to the count of five.

"No. I think I'll be all right. Let's proceed." She extracted her hands from Luna's.

"You are safe here. If at any time you want to stop or just take a break, let me know. This is for you and you set the tone. Remember, it's all about you," Luna said, shifting until she was directly next to Alicia.

"Thank you. I appreciate you. I had started what I thought was my own therapy—trips around the world—those didn't heal the ache inside."

Luna held her gaze and said, "You didn't deserve what happened to you and it wasn't your fault."

Tears welled up and spilled down Alicia's cheeks, and she nodded. "I always blamed myself. If only I hadn't done this or hadn't said that," she said, plucking a few tissue from the blue and white box next to her seat.

"The blame stops with the people who abused you," Luna countered."

Alicia lowered her head and nodded.

"You've been carrying around guilt and shame that do not belong to you, but to those who violated you. That's a heavy burden for anyone to suffer, more so for a child."

The conversation continued and Alicia became more comfortable and responsive as the session progressed. They covered several incidents relating to childhood sexual and physical abuse and traumatic episodes with her husband in adulthood.

About two hours later Luna brought the session to a close by saying, "Alicia, you are worthy of love, happiness and peace. You'll get there."

Alicia stood, placed the water bottle on the side table, moved passed Luna and stood in front of the water fountain, gazing at the ripples cascading down the wall while listening to the sounds.

Luna remained seated, silent, observing her client and new friend. After several minutes passed, she came to Alicia's side her gaze also fixed on the crystal clear water rolling down to the pool below. "How are you feeling this minute?"

Alicia took a few moments before she responded, "I'm feeling great. I just wish Dallas was here to know that I've taken the first steps." She then retrieved her phone frantically typed a message, smiled, and hit send.

Chapter 14

"Kamran *is* now being considered Crown Prince," Sheikh Aayan announced as he closed the door behind the last dignitary who attended the peace meeting with Nadaum.

Amir's neck snapped around like a bobblehead and he almost lost his balance as his foot collided with the chair he was about to vacate. Kamran flinched; the news was a complete surprise to him as well.

"What, are you out of your mind, father?" The dethroned Crown Prince questioned.

The Sheikh scowled and rose to his feet. "Are you questioning my judgement?" He bellowed and violently shoved the chair towards the desk.

"He is too weak to lead. Our people are going to laugh at us. He couldn't even produce an heir with the two wives you procured." Prince

Amir exclaimed, his brows knitted, and his lips twisted, as he stepped backwards to create distance between himself and his father.

The Sheikh remained silent as he shot a dagger stare at Amir, then raised his right arm and pointed to the door, "Out, now. When I give an order, no questions should follow. Out!"

Amir shot Kamran a look of contempt and stormed out of the room, the fire in his eyes signaled hellraising would soon follow.

Kamran's mind quickly went to the plans he could implement before his father had another change of heart and replace him.

All I need is one week.

Time enough to secure the women's shelter and declare it off limits to any attack. Time enough to … He wouldn't be able to do away with El Zalaam, but he could mandate charges if the women were found to be underage or there against their will.

The Sheikh returned to his chair and slammed his hand on the desk.

Kamran returned to the present and stood near the bookcase facing his father. Memories of the past few years crashed through his mind and threatened to drown him, and he swallowed hard and took long deep breaths. He had been the laughingstock of the family when he failed to sire children with his wives, who eventually left and bore children with other husbands.

Now, another change of fortune. But he knew it was only temporary. Father was angry at Amir for the moment. When that subsided, another declaration would follow.

He turned to his father, his forehead pinched and lips moving, but no words escaped.

"I have faith in you son, you will be an exceptional leader of Durabia when the time comes," Sheikh Aayan informed him with a sly grin.

Kamran turned his head away. "It is a lot to take in, yes," he replied, remembering the angry look on his younger brother's face as he left the room.

Despite everyone's knowledge that he could not influence his father's decisions, this would ripple into more underhandedness by his brothers to win their father's affection.

Chapter 15

This is going to be a long night.

Dallas felt lost and alone, pacing from the dining room, to the living room to gaze through the window of Luna's condo. He was totally on board with the plan to ensure Alicia's safety but wished it hadn't meant separating them. His face broke out into a smile when his cellphone screen lit up and he read her message.

I love you and miss you so much. I want this nightmare to be over.

"Me too," he responded and pulled up a picture of the latest *People's* Magazine cover with Dallas smiling for the camera. The paparazzi had snapped the perfect shot this time. But it wasn't the one the man intended. Thanks to Alicia's quick movements, the camera did not capture a full-on image of her. He thought of her and the amazing person she was, loving, generous, and compassionate and wanted to ensure her privacy as much as possible.

Dallas quickly switched to Face Time, dialed and Alicia quickly connected. His heart ached as he noticed combined with the bright smile were mist of tears on her lashes.

"How are you, baby?" he asked softly, kissing her face through the screen.

He saw her pout and kissed back. "I'm hanging in there, my love," she said, he saw a tear rolled down one cheek as the connection ended. He stared at the blank screen for a while, thinking of her and reminding himself how lucky and blessed he was for having her in his life.

One of their most recent discussions popped to mind. They had been discussing charitable donations and he mentioned that one of his former teammates was in need of help.

"Michael Green?" She had exclaimed when he mentioned the name.

He had explained that Michael needed assistance for drug rehab and that it would be a good idea to include him as one of their charitable donations. "I told him I would have to discuss it with you." She was his unofficial financial advisor and all major expenses had to pass her sniffing test. She had listened intently as he laid out the details of his talk with Michael.

Alicia recalled some of the sad news reports about Michael—him being arrested for drug possession and beaten and robbed on the streets and expressed sympathy for him.

"Yes, like a lot of other professional athletes, he had made a lot of money, but it left him like water through a basket." Dallas responded.

At the end of the conversation, she replied, "Let's make it happen, and we will pray for him too. Sometimes a higher power is needed along with that cash."

He pulled her in his arms, tilted her chin, and his lips and tongue slowly massaged across her lips. Alicia responded in kind, and as their tongues danced, the rhythm accelerated, and heat spread throughout their bodies. His hands strolled across her face, to her neck down her shoulders and back. He lifted her dress and cupped her buttocks, only to discover that it was bare. Message sent and received, and his animal side took over. His fingers dived lower and landed in her juices and he let out a throaty growl. He started to lift her towards the bed, but she held up her hand, signaling for him to wait. Alicia felt the hardness of his manhood knocking on her abdomen, begging for release, and clawed at this zipper to set it free. She then knelt at his feet and guided his member into her mouth for a playful, passionate exploration.

He moaned, as her lips and tongue searched and found the pleasure spots—in and out, up, and down and all around. While she teased and thrilled, he guided her head in the direction he wanted her to move, until he felt as if he would explode. With the speed of a cheetah, he lifted her, carried her to the bed and returned the favor. It seemed he enlisted his entire skillset to stimulate her pearl, and in response she thrusts her hips to match the movements. He drank from her fountain, until he felt the crescendo, then sat up and dove in deep and hard. She accepted and returned every thrust with equal gusto and passion. They climaxed together and clung to one another so tightly, the desire reignited, and signaled a repeat.

She brings so much joy to my life.

He moved away from the window, the memory invoked feelings and desires he couldn't entertain, not today anyway.

"Alicia," he whispered. "I have to get her out of here and soon."

Chapter 16

"Father, I need to speak with you," Prince Amir said as he barged into the office, his eye on Kamran who tucked a set of papers into a brown business case as if not wanting Amir to see them.

The royal office of Sheikh Aayan was fitted with an extravagant brown wooden desk adorned with gold accents and carvings interlay and trimmings, flanked by high back beige chairs with gold accents, pictures of family, and special awards adorned the walls, a large screen apple computer sat in the center and connected to multiple screens.

The Sheikh glowered at him the moment Amir dropped down into a seat, making himself comfortable. "You entered without knocking? We are in a private meeting. Wait until I summon you." He shoved his chair back and towered over Amir while lifting a palm towards him.

Kamran was the most, if not the only, honorable one of the Sheikh's sons and was highly respected at home and abroad. His brother's plots to hinder him from occupying the Durabian throne had not affected his plan to give Durabia a make-over, especially in the area of safety and security for women. His passion for uplifting women, particularly those being trafficked and housed at El Zalaam and at the women's shelter had always been at the forefront of his humanitarian efforts. He was intolerant of those who patronized El Zalaam, even those men within the palace, who thought of it as a private matter. He vowed to sign a decree to shield the shelter from attacks and outside influence and to remove the ugly scar of sex trafficking as soon as he was in a position to do so.

With his eyes fixed on Kamran, Amir ignored the warning and stood. "Father, as Crown Prince, I should be present at these meetings because I should be aware of everything," Amir said as he looked up at his father, struggling to keep his feelings from showing on his face.

"Crown Prince?" his father's voice had increased by a hundred decibels and everyone in the room shrank back as his eyes flashed daggers at Amir. "Your standing is in question right now. We will see about that. Your actions, both here and abroad, are despicable. You bring shame to the Palace wherever you go. You had better hope that Nadaum only forces an arranged marriage with the child you accosted. Leave my office now!"

"How was I to know she was a royal?" Amir responded.

Kamran scoffed and said, "No issues with her being a child though."

"You stay out of this," Amir warned. "Thanks to you, all of us are under fire."

'I was there when father received the call about your recent trip to Nadaum. Wherever you go you cannot keep your qadib to yourself. You have to find a woman, no matter what. Your relentless appetite for sex landed you in relations with a barely past teen woman, who happened to be an immediate member of the royal family in Nadaum. Then you tried to make a secret deal with the son of the family's advocate which unraveled the moment the victim told what you had done. Now there is a bounty on your head. The relationship between the palace and Nadaum is in chaos and father is still engaged in negotiations to restore their partnership."

Sheikh Aayan nodded at the truth of Kamran's words.

"Father, you have to stop accommodating him and shielding him from trouble." Kamran said as he glared at Amir.

The Sheikh walked past Amir and opened the door, raised his right arm, and extended his index finger outside.

Chapter 14

The next morning, Alicia dressed in a pair of black leggings underneath a green and purple thawb, slipped her feet into a pair of tan-colored sandals and stepped out to join the other women for breakfast.

"I still can't believe you're one of us," Lia said, taking her hand, and guiding her towards the other women.

Luna strolled up and patted her shoulder, and Alicia turned towards Lia and said, "If you only knew. If you only knew my story."

Other women came forward and greeted her, hugging, and shaking hands. Alicia returned the greetings and matched pace to the dining room.

"What are we doing today, Agent Xeva?" She leaned in and whispered so only Luna could hear, and continued walking.

Luna's step faltered but recovered quickly she hadn't been called that since leaving the military and she wondered at the use of it right now and continued in step with the group. "I sometimes take the women to the mall in small groups. But I don't think an outing is the right thing to do right now. It's best if we remain here and interact with the women until we know what's going on."

Keep our guards up.

The shelter was the brainchild of some of the influential women in Durabia who had grown tired of witnessing abuses in their homes, plus others in the community and of the women being trafficked at El Zalaam, where most of their husbands, including some housed in the palace receive their wanton fill. They had connected with Luna about one year after she arrived in Durabia. They discovered Luna's work from one of the women whom she had been working with and visited her home. By the time they called she had heard of the shelter and the work being done there.

Luna's bi-weekly visits to the shelter included individual and group therapy sessions in addition to self-defense classes. The women blossomed under her care and Alicia fitted seamlessly into the activities.

The success of the shelter was mostly due to its support by people in the Palace, especially Prince Kamran Ali Khan.

"Miss Evangelista, we would love for you to join with us and use your talents to further help these women." One of the women, Aisha had informed her, "these women need you; we have saved many and some have even been reunited with their families in other countries." She continued in a pleading tone.

Luna had agreed without hesitation and a partnership was forged where she would provide weekly counseling at the shelter, to include self-defense training.

Chapter 18

"Front desk with delivery for Mr. Avery."

Dallas quickly unfolded his frame from the sofa, raised an eyebrow, paused, looked at his phone, then hesitantly walked to the door and peeked through the keyhole. His eye landed on the bellhop he met in the elevator the night they arrived.

How does anyone know where I am?

He cautiously opened the door, leaving the safety chain engaged and peered through the crack. "How may I help you," he asked, fixing his gaze on the young man.

"I have a delivery for you, sir," he said, shoving a white envelope towards Dallas, while turning to the side preparing for departure.

"Thank you," Dallas said, as he grasped the envelope, closed the door, slid the lock into place and a pulse beat at his temple.

The Crown Prince? What the hell?

He ripped open the envelope—An Invitation.

The Crown Prince of Durabia cordially invites Mr. Avery and Ms. Mitchell to the Royal Palace to join the family for dinner at a date to be determined.

The Prince is an avid basketball fan, especially of Mr. Avery...

Dallas stopped reading; his eyes flickered shut as memories of the Prince gawking at Alicia crashed to the forefront of his mind. He thought of Alicia, opened his eyes, slapped the envelope onto the dining table, chest puffed out and chin lifted, he raised his cellphone and dialed, while pacing to gaze out the window across the horizons, his vision unfocused.

This man wants Alicia as bad as I do.

* * *

Alone in a strange house and country Dallas pulled out his computer and hit up google. The Royal Family of Durabia was the subject line. He quickly discovered that Amir was one of the many sons that Sheikh Aayan spawned through his six wives and with the exception of Kamran, the others were not well liked or respected worldwide.

Kamran, who was once Crown Prince, lost the title when he failed to produce any children with his two wives who later left him, married other men, and bore children. The brothers all disliked Kamran and often joined heads to curry favor their father against him and individually plotted against each other to win their father's favor.

The brothers, except Kamran, were rumored to be frequent visitors to El Zalaam, where some of the women were underage and others held against their will.

Wow, even the women were causing a stir.

One of the wives and two daughters had defected and sought asylum in Europe. If the latest headlines were to be believed, Nadaum officials were gunning for Amir, although the reason was not publicly revealed.

That's why the little coward was on the flight from Chicago. He was hiding.

Chapter 10

"We'll rest up tonight, follow up on intel tomorrow and get you and Dallas out of the country. How about that?" Luna nudged Alicia.

"If we have no other choice." Alicia stopped speaking at the ring from Luna's phone.

Luna stared down at the number and frowned. Dallas Avery. *Why was he calling her instead of Alicia? He probably dialed the wrong number.*

Expecting it to be a misdial, she glanced at Alicia and answered, "Dallas."

"I hope you're sitting down. You need to for what I'm going to tell you," he said in a rushed tone.

Every time anyone tells her to sit, she knew it would be bad news. As a matter of fact, the last time, was ten years ago, and it was to inform her that her favorite aunt had died.

She raised her fingers to touch the pulse throbbing at her throat as if to prevent her heart from escaping. "Let it out, Dallas." She looked over at Alicia and stepped closer to where she was sitting on the edge of the center table in the living room.

"I received an invitation to the Palace from Crown Prince Amir for us to join him. How did he know where we were staying?"

"Repeat?" Clearly she hadn't heard him correctly.

"Yes, it was delivered directly to your condo by the bellhop."

She held the phone away from her ears and looked at Alicia. She gulped for air and leaned over on the table and holding on with her free hand.

"Are you all right?" Alicia sprang to her side and grabbed the phone from her hand.

"Dear Lord. I…" Her eyes misted, with the ramifications of what this could mean.

"Luna!" Dallas' voice echoed through the phone.

Alicia looked at Luna, then to the phone. "Dallas, she'll call you back shortly."

The Prince knew where they were staying.

'There is no way," she whispered.

Who in her circle would betray them?

"What's going on?" Alicia asked, as she placed the cellphone on the sofa table and stood facing her.

Luna lowered her gaze, grabbed a bottle of water, and turned it upside down in her mouth. She was still trying to come to grips with the implication of the call. She thought of how carefully she had planned and set up her location and had kept it secluded to protect all involved. Her contacts were trustworthy, or so she thought. She didn't want to believe that this was true.

"The Crown Prince knows where I live and that you and Dallas are staying there."

"What?" Alicia let out a sharp gasp. "How?"

"I've been betrayed." A sentence she never thought she had to utter, ever. There had to be another explanation. She slowly walked to the couch and slumped into it. "I don't know who or how, but I sure as hell am going to find out."

Betrayal could be deadly.

The survivor network was secretive, secured and well connected to individuals and organizations in Durabia who were passionate about the welfare of the women it served. Prince Kamran Ali Kahn was its highest-level supporter and when far reaching assistance is required he was the go-to man.

Now was one of those times.

Chapter 20

Amir sat in the royal palace theatre and as he scanned the room's décor his mind prickled with the memory of his latest trip to Nadaum. He had been out with friends who always provided him with every available luxury and supplied him with a woman or few when he visited. This one was younger than usual and a real beauty. Like the others, she was eager to please him believing she would be elevated in status by becoming his wife. And please him she did. He closed his eyes and a picture flashed across his mind. He hadn't asked for credentials. He never did. Never had to. That was for the peasants of the world.

The following day he received word that she was a member of the royal family. His friend, the son of the family's advocate, quickly accepted the payment he offered and secured Amir's immediate departure by driving him to a private jet. Plans were underway to ask for his father's help to quash any possible issue that would arise. Only problem, things didn't work out. The advocate kept the money and the girl had reported the events to her father.

The ringing cell phone diverted his attention from the ocean-deep thoughts and saved him from sinking under the weight of his father's wrath.

"We are in position, sir," Nasir relayed as he motioned to the others to await his signal to begin the operation.

They'd heard whispers of this place but had never felt the need to investigate or enter until now. "Miss Evangelista and her accomplices have been snatching the women from El Zalaam and denying men their fleshly pleasures. Now we will let them know who is in charge as we take control and add the beautiful Alicia Mitchell to the lot."

Prince Amir will be delighted. Nasir's mouth watered in anticipation of the raise and status upgrade in the palace he would gain at the end of this task. And if things worked out well, he would also be granted full access to the girls and women who had been placed out of reach long before the royals had tired of them.

"Great job, my friend," the Prince exclaimed as he settled in the palace theatre with legs apart hand resting near his qadib, which was throbbing with excitement. "I cannot wait to experience what I have heard about in those sexy American magazines. American women can do amazing things in the bedroom."

Nasir reminisced about the time he first met the man who had unwillingly granted him access to the shelter. They were both members of the same circle and often communed. However, the man was tight-lipped about what he did for a living and where he went at certain times. Nasir had become suspicious and followed him. Threats to harm his family and bribes had the man singing like a bird. A few days later, access to the building and its occupants were within their reach.

"Are you sure we can get in?" He had asked the man, doubting that entry could be so easy. Especially after all this time and no demands from the palace had achieved desirable results. Kamran Ali Khan had covered this place as some sort of a guardian angel.

"Yes, I am sure," the man responded and hung his head with shame.

Prince Amir waited for the call that never came. Trying to reach Nasir sent him straight to voicemail.

His anger grew and patience wore thin. He couldn't reconcile his father's current action of having, Kamran, of all people, to replace him. The man didn't know how to rule if leadership smacked him upside the head.

Disappointment and frustration took control and he stood to leave, just then his phone rang, and he quickly answered.

"This is Syed Hassan, Military Officer who reports to Sheikh Aayan. We have arrested four men who say they work for you. We are coming to the palace for you to answer a few questions. We expect your father to be present."

With those three sentences Amir felt the throne permanently slide out of reach as he stuttered "W-h-a-t did you say?"

Chapter 21

Luna rushed into the day room where the women gathered for group therapy, her gaze instantly locked on Alicia. Her heart beat thunderously and beads of perspiration dotted on her forehead.

"Ladies, we have to move," she shouted, grabbing Alicia by the arm. "We have a security breach. Follow the guards to the steel room like we practiced." She pointed to the three guards standing in the doorway.

Gun in hand, Luna beckoned to the group and placed a finger to her lips for silence. As the other women trailed the guards, she turned to Alicia. "Do you know how to use a gun?"

Her eyes widened and she breathed deeply. "Yes, but knives are my specialty."

"Good, take these." Luna pulled a Glock 43 from a black military backpack and handed it over, accompanied by a sheathed Ka-Bar military knife.

Alicia felt a slight thrill mingled with terror and she pressed her body to the wall. "I'll be damned if I'm going to roll over and play man's best friend. I know this is happening because of me." She directed a steady look at Luna.

"There are only three guards here and you've met them already. Anyone who enters the building you don't recognize, shoot. If their face is covered, shoot. If you're in doubt about the identity, shoot. Shoot to kill, we'll sort it out later."

Alicia nodded, saddened that she had brought this danger to such a beautiful and peaceful place.

She followed close behind Luna down the long hallway. As they passed a half-opened door, a hand slid out and pulled Alicia inside, and the door softly closed behind her. She got a quick glimpse of a face that reminded her of Antonio Banderas in The Mask of Zorro.

He snatched the Glock from her hand and her head hit the wall hard as rough hands shoved her then covered her mouth to muffle the screams. Stars flashed in her vision field and dizziness took over. Before she could recover, he grabbed her hair, spun around and with a quick movement she was chest pressed, bottoms up against the brown wooden table. Nausea and the taste of bile rose into her mouth.

Alicia's pulse quickened, and her breathing came in short bursts. She shuddered at the memories that surfaced from her childhood, reminding her of the times grown men tried to violate her, as if she didn't have the right to say no, as if she didn't own her body, or that consent of a child was *implied*. At eight. Nine. Ten. She pushed the memories back and forced herself to remain calm and breathe. As he fumbled with his clothing, she whispered, "I know you'll kill me after you're done, so let me see your face. I need to see who is about to take something from me knowing I haven't given consent."

He paused and burst out laughing. "Consent is not my concern. Not even Mr. NBA can help you now."

Like Jesus in the temple with the money changers, righteous indignation rose up in Alicia. She frowned, jaws clenched, perspiration streaming down her forehead, and her face became flushed.

Not today. Not this body. Enough! One of us is going to die.

With cheetah-like speed, she turned, pushed him backwards and reached down to her boots, grabbed the Ka-Bar and in a quick motion, plunged deep into his left chest. His eyes widened with shock and his mouth opened, but the only sound that came was gurgling blood. She pushed him backwards and he slid off the knife and plopped backwards to the floor.

No more! No more!

She wiped the knife on his pants, returned it to her boot, then went to check for a pulse. The slight creaking of the door grabbed her attention. Alicia snatched the Glock from the floor, heart pounding and breathing rapidly, as an unfamiliar figure advanced towards her. Luna's voice resonated in her head, "Shoot."

She watched as his strides closed the distance between them, aimed her gun and heard a solid *pop*. Before she could blink once, his body hit hers like an eighteen-wheeler barreling forward at full speed. Their bodies hit the floor with a loud thud and the Glock fell from her hand and scattered across the wood floor. The pressure on Alicia's chest felt as though a skyscraper had fallen on her.

"You should've had better aim." He reached his thick hands around her neck.

She slammed both hands against his, fighting to loosen his vice grip. The fight or flight hormone was in full control as Alicia fought to breathe and escape or at least move her leg enough to reach the Ka-Bar. The pressure on her throat was threatening to take her out. Her fingertips just managed to touch the handle of the knife.

Her body stilled. He loosened his grip slightly seconds before she plunged the blade into his back. She kneed him in the groin as he shifted to touch the stab wound before she raced for the door. Loud voices coming from all directions and what sounded like bursts of gunfire outdoors greeted her as she dashed in the hallway.

Alicia glanced back to see him lunging a moment too late. He yanked her ankle causing her to hit the ground. Alicia's hands scratched against the floor trying to slow the backward momentum.

She shoved a boot hard into his mouth, then drove the knife into his upper chest. His hand flew to the open wound as the coppery scent of blood penetrated the air. Just then Luna and one guard raced around the corner to her left.

"Alicia?" Luna hurried to her side with her weapon aimed at the man still gasping on the ground. "Are you injured?"

"No." Alicia glanced down at the bloody clothes and touched her throat.

Luna glanced in the room at the other body stretched out on the floor. "You're a badass." She gently pulled her away from the now subdued captive.

"I wouldn't say that, but, I knew I had to defend myself. Thank God for rescuing me," she declared as the guard moved forward to secure the intruder.

Sirens blasted outdoors and military boots trampled the hallways.

"How are you, really?" Luna enquired; concern etched in her expression.

Alicia could only nod and signal for her to follow. When they reached the destination, Alicia opened the door and pointed inside.

Luna gasped and stepped back. "What is Zahri doing here?"

Chapter 22

Luna stared, shocked at the familiar body sprawled on the floor with blood gushing from his chest.

Her trusted driver.

She placed her right hand to her belly and sank to the floor. *How did he come to be involved? Was his wife, Khadija and family safe? Especially Khadija, who was one of her clients, a survivor of sexual and domestic violence before she met Zahri. Now he'd never be able to answer those questions.*

All of her challenging work and that of the people in the community who cared for the women they rescued. The chatter and shuffling of feet faded away and the only sound echoing was her heart being ripped into thousands of little pieces.

What now?

Alicia walked over and placed a hand under one elbow to assist her to a standing position.

Tears streamed down her cheeks as she walked over to the sofa and collapsed, head in her hands and the sobs rocked her body.

Alicia stood off to the side as several officers quickly entered the room and secured the scene. She stepped outside in the hallway where more officers spread throughout the center while Luna wrapped her mind around everything that transpired.

Several minutes later, Alicia returned to extract Luna and they left to meet with the lead officer and give a statement. After they were finished, Luna fetched the women from the steel room and contacted her network to begin the transfer to the backup location and alert Prince Kamran.

Luna had the women sitting in the therapy room practicing some relaxation techniques as they waited. Understandably, they were still reeling from the shock, but enthusiastically committed to the routine. They were determined to continue their healing journey—no matter where it took place.

"Survivors," they shouted in one voice.

The door burst opened, and a group of men walked in led by Crown Prince Kamran Ali Khan, along with a few members of the Durabian council who had no clue of what was about to transpire. His father was absent and secluded in a meeting with the Sheikh of Nadaum which gave Kamran this once in a lifetime opportunity to further his own cause of making Durabia safe for women of all walks of life, no matter if they were nationals, tourists, or ex-pats.

Kamran stepped forward and addressed the group. "Today we all join and proclaim that the women's shelter is a safe space and therefore off limits to any interference from the outside, and by nationals and royalty alike. We will have specially trained female guards stationed here to replace all palace and military security personnel." Those who came all nodded.

He handed the Proclamation to Luna that had been executed by his hand, and the council members reluctantly put their pen to paper. She held it up to show the women who erupted with cheers.

As she left the building under the protection of Kamran's guards, Alicia's only thought was, *where's Dallas*.

They pulled the front door open and before she could fully step foot outside, Dallas rushed forward and wrapped his arms around her. She buried her face in his chest and sobbed.

"Let's get out of here," he mouthed against her ear as he looked down at his vibrating cell phone.

"Stay away from the airport for now," Luna cautioned as the group strode towards one of the vehicles.

Chapter 23

Prince Amir's henchmen had the airport under surveillance. Dallas and one of his military officers remained in the vehicle near the entrance to the mall to work out a plan while Alicia and Luna, dressed in traditional Arabian attire, entered the mall escorted by two military officers dressed in brown dishdashi and sandals, and blended in with the day's shoppers.

The trip to the mall was fascinating—the colors, smells—overall captivating. Since they were to spend time and act like tourists Luna had educated Alicia on the ins and outs of shopping. Negotiating was a must—there was always a lower price. Luna had to remind her this wasn't Souk. She could try but they were less likely to budge. With the events at the shelter foremost on her mind, Alicia stepped up to one of the stalls where one of the women was selling Pashminas and bargained. The test of her bartering skills yielded great results, so she was empowered and willed herself to proceed. Similar deals were achieved during her encounter with sellers of Durabian garb, for her and Dallas. Midway through the adventure they were so laden down with packages she wasn't sure how this would make it home.

"That's beautiful." Alicia gestured to the assorted coats on a nearby rack and hurried over. She reached for a beautiful scarlet red, double breasted, below-knee length raincoat, with notched lapels, cinched waist, slipped it on over her clothing, and twirled in front of the display mirror. Satisfied with the look, she reached for the matching umbrella on an adjacent stand, and finalized the purchase. A radiant smile graced her face. *Another one to my collection.*

Alicia did her best to give the impression she had forgotten where she was and what had transpired earlier. With laughter, joking with the salespeople, and making light conversations. It seemed to please Luna to observe how relaxed and giddy Alicia appeared at times as if she was an Academy Award actress performing a role.

"Let's take some of these bags to the car then grab something to eat," Luna announced, as she placed some of the bags on the floor and gave her arms a long stretch and shake.

"I'll continue shopping until you return." Alicia announced as she turned towards another saleswoman and held up a gold and brown Pashmina.

"We should stay together," she remarked and retrieved the bags from the floor. Luna took the item from her hand, held her arm, and urged her to follow which she did without hesitation and the officers shadowed at a discreet distance.

Prince Amir, the scene playing out in the Durabian airport parking lot, and the past kidnappings replayed in her mind. "I know. Although I love shopping, it was a little hard focusing in there. I won't feel safe until I'm home with Dallas"

From Scotland, Canada, and God knows the other places, everywhere she travelled somebody was waiting to snatch her out of Dallas' arms. Someone was there to give her hell and make her life miserable. So far she had been rescued or escaped herself each time. But for how long.

When will my luck run out?

"I'm starving," Luna declared while handing over money for one last purchase and shoved the bright pink pashmina into her bag. "Maybe we should grab something to eat first."

They made their way to the ground floor to explore the many food choices. A brief description of FIG Ristorante on the display piqued their interest. Hungry shoppers crowded the place, due to the time of day, and the fact that the mall was packed with people from all over the world. Since all the inside tables were occupied, they went out on the terrace, where they had to share table with two other female diners.

Although crowded, the terrace presented sophisticated classiness and amazing views of the Durabian Fountain—stylish, but informal and FIG offered fine Italian cuisine infused with local spices.

Alicia sensed they were being watched, but a brief survey of the scene around them, didn't reveal anyone of interest except their escorts. "We should go now."

They left behind their lunch untouched.

"That was different from what I normally do," Luna muttered as they pushed their way through the crowd across the dining room and reentered the shopping area of the mall. "I don't usually mingle with the crowds when I'm out with the women but wanted to make sure we didn't attract any unwanted attention."

A group of people forced their way between her and Luna. Alicia fought to catch sight of Luna or their escorts as more bodies separated them. Panic set in as she made her way to a less populated area. Alicia kept scanning the area looking for Luna or the escorts when she noticed two menacing men approaching.

She bolted in the direction of the of the stairs leading to the upper level with the men zig-zagging through the pedestrian traffic right along with her. Her eyes frantically searched the faces hoping to catch sight of Luna or one of their escorts. Two steps at a time, Alicia made her way to the upper level with arms burning and heart racing as they closed the distance between them.

Would they really try to snatch her from a heavily populated area?

Alicia wasn't waiting to find out as she hustled to the exit. Alicia moved most of the bags to one hand so that she could throw one of them to maintain distance if needed. As she turned to look over her left shoulder, a hand grabbed her right arm. Alicia swung a bag in the that direction planning on going down fighting.

Dallas blocked the hit with an arm. "It's me."

She lowered her arm as relief flooded her soul. "You scared me," Alicia said, finally noticing Luna and the two guards standing several feet behind him.

"I'll get the ladies out of here." Dallas glanced at the two military men. "You take care of them."

He nodded towards the men now retreating in the opposite direction.

As they left the mall, Alicia silently glanced over at Luna and squeezed her hand as Dallas carried their bags out.

"I was so scared for you when we couldn't find you." Luna locked gazes and squeezed back.

"You weren't the only one."

They returned to the vehicle, stowed the bags, and strapped in.

Dallas kissed her temple. "This is almost over."

Alicia nestled close to Dallas and his arm snaked around her shoulders and pulled her close.

"We are ready to head to the airport." An officer revved the engine, mashed the pedal and the vehicle slowly merged into ongoing traffic.

"Sweetest words I've heard since we arrived in this place," Dallas exclaimed, and Alicia nodded.

Chapter 24

Kamran rushed up the palace steps, gaze sweeping the area as he advanced. He was still riding on cloud nine about the success of the shelter visit and that the women were now completely protected no matter who sat on the throne. There was nothing that could be done to reverse course because Proclamations were absolute. One pressing item remained on his list of things to accomplish.

Now that Alicia and Luna had flushed out the last of the threat with their shopping excursion, he felt confident that there was only one more thing to take care of. He walked briskly through the passageway, past the throne room, and into the palace theatre, forward until he spotted the person he was seeking.

A lone figure stood with his head bowed and his back towards the door.

Kamran tapped his brother on the shoulder and spoke in a harsh tone as he pushed him forward. "Do not speak. Just do what I tell you."

Amir hesitated but complied and gasped when their eyes met.

Kamran held an index finger to his lips and shook his head several times.

"W-h-a-t?" Amir's shoulders slumped.

After a silent exchange, Amir quietly moved in the direction where he was being shoved. They went past a row of decorated tables and continued toward the hallway, then through the secret passage into the parking lot lined with luxury SUVs and cars.

The dark-gray SUV parked at the curb with doors ajar seemed to beckon them. Four tall men leaned against it; arms folded across their middle.

Kamran stopped at the rear driver's side door and pushed Amir inside. The other men entered and secured their seat belts. With a wave of one hand and a silent command from Kamran, the vehicle passed through the gates and merged into traffic.

Flanked by his personal bodyguards, Kamran followed at a distance. He didn't need to be at the airport, but after everything that had been done, he was eager to see the back end of Amir on his way to face the consequences of his actions.

Ten minutes later, the SUV rolled up to a secluded private airstrip. As the vehicle came near the lone airplane that had its engine running, a man wearing a white dishdasha stepped out of the hangar. He hurried to the plane and stood waiting as the hem of his dishdasha swirled in the wind.

As soon as the vehicle stopped, all the doors opened, and the security detail escorted a struggling Amir toward the plane.

Kamran's SUV rolled onto the tarmac, and he watched from the back seat, a few feet away with the window slightly lowered.

"Don't waste your energy, Amir," the man in the white dishdasha warned as they approached him.

As recognition set in, Amir grunted and fought harder.

The man clamped a hand on Amir's left shoulder and squeezed.

Seconds later, Amir's body went limp, and the others carried him up the steps and deposited him inside the plane.

"Do not worry about him." Tipping his head toward the aircraft, he added, "He will sleep all the way to Nadaum."

"My regards to Crown Prince Kamran Ali Khan. Please tell him I look forward to renewing relations between Nadaum and Durabia. With this offering Sheikh Zoraib will be pleased and vindicated." The soldier handed over a sealed, white envelope.

Kamran had seen enough. As the airplane door closed, he commanded the chauffeur to leave. Behind him, the airplane taxied down the runway.

After ten minutes, his phone vibrated, and he looked at the screen. He opened the message icon and read the text.

We will keep our promise not to kill him.

No, Amir will face a second marriage of the Nadaum sheikh's choosing. Something Amir absolutely had avoided at all costs. He swiped up and the screen closed. As he stared through the window, he thought about how Amir had forced his hand. As the ruling party, he would always have difficult decisions to make. This one was no different. Their father would be upset that he had a hand in this, but would surely understand that at times a great leader will be forced to place the interest of country ahead of those of family. Especially family that keeps doing all manner of evil.

Sorry father, it had to be done.

Chapter 25

As her breath misted in the crisp morning air, Alicia draped a knee-length black coat around her body and dashed a quick glance behind her as she walked beside Dallas to the check in counter at the Durabian airport, again.

"I can't wait to get out of here," she said, noticing a tall, well-built, strikingly handsome man with olive skin accompanied by two similar looking escorts advancing towards then.

Dallas turned at the sound of her voice, held and squeezed her hand then followed her gaze and his eyes fixed on the men.

"They told us the coast was clear for us to leave." The concern was evident in his voice and matched what she felt.

His steps quickened. The tallest of the group reached them first and held up his right hand. Alicia and Dallas stopped and stepped backwards. *Not again.*

"Do not be alarmed Mr. Avery and Ms. Mitchell."

"Give me one reason why we shouldn't be." Dallas snapped, shoulders pulled back and his chin pointed upward, while pulling Alicia closer to his body and slightly behind him with one of his feet positioned forward in a protective stance.

He held out his right hand to Dallas. "I am Crown Prince Kamran Ali Khan, and I would like you to remain in Durabia as my guest. I want you to experience all the good things we have to offer and not leave with a negative opinion based on the unsavory actions of my brother."

Dallas' face relaxed as he finally recognized the man who coordinated their escape, but his grip on Alicia intensified. "You're the good son." He hesitantly shook the outstretched hand as if the filth from Amir might be familial.

"I am so sorry, Miss Mitchell, please let me make it up to you. I am inviting you to my residence for as long as you wish to stay."

Alicia sighed and there was a world of emotions in that one sound.

"Sir, I just want to get my woman the hell out of here before anyone else gets ideas," Dallas responded his eyes lasering on Kamran.

Kamran nodded. "I understand, Mr. Avery. However, your safety is guaranteed from here onwards."

"Really? Where is that bad seed, Amir?" Dallas queried, his lips tightened.

Kamran flickered a gaze from Dallas to Alicia, then to the two men who were with him, and folded his arms across his chest. "Let me just say, he has been taken care of."

The tone said everything.

"I would've preferred to take care of the bastard myself," Dallas added, his eyes glowing with anger.

Kamran took in the well-placed hostility directed at his brother. He ran from Nadaum to distance himself from the dastardly deeds he committed there, only to become embodied with something even more nefarious, by trying to take Miss Mitchell.

He stretched a hand towards Alicia who grasped it and smiled.

"Please call me Alicia."

Chapter 26

Five days at Kamran's private residence had been great for Alicia. Peaceful. Amazing. Kamran lived up to his word even though doing so had cost him on a personal level. Sheikh Aayan was angered at what had been done with Amir and the safety net placed around the women who found their way out of El Zalaam and into Luna's network. The nationals and wealthy tourists alike were in an uproar over Kamran's action. He was no longer the Crown Prince, nor would he ever be considered.

The bad feelings and dreams about the ordeal in Durabia were fading along with others that had transpired over their ninety days of adventure. She sensed that it had to be because she was with Dallas, her knight wrapped in a six foot-plus package delivering endless love and joy. She always felt safe and secure in his arms and was now learning to love herself even more.

What is life if you aren't with the person you love? Should I take that chance?

Additionally, she had continued her therapy sessions with Luna, which had helped her to start breathing freely again and enjoying her time with Dallas in Durabia. She was finally cancelling the subscription she held for the fear of trusting, lack of selflove, low self-esteem and the fear of being loved.

Alicia's last session with Luna was brief and took place by the outdoor water fountain at Kamran's residence. She and Luna had made a good connection and the sessions had progressed more than they had initially anticipated. Luna reinforced the various techniques that would be used going forward—affirmations, breathing exercises, positive self-talk, daily journaling, and specific books to read.

"As I mentioned in our previous sessions, this is a journey that will take some time," Luna said, fixing her gaze on Alicia. "We will continue our work via video feed when you return to the States."

Alicia nodded. "I look forward to that."

"Please take the remainder of the time you have in Durabia to be with Dallas and get some rest and relaxation." Luna held her hand and they walked back into the house.

* * *

She was stretched out on her side and from behind Dallas wrapped his arms around her and she snuggled back into him. Her gaze landed on the twenty-carat diamond ring he had placed on her left ring finger the day before. The gorgeous three-stone diamond ring displayed two 5.2 carat side diamonds and was designed to stand out and make everyone take notice. They had been out shopping at the Durabian Mall enjoying the hospitality generously offered by the Crown Prince. He had also held an audience with them on ways he could improve Durabia's financial and social infrastructure.

Alicia smiled as she recalled the moment Dallas had placed it on her finger. He had gently guided her to the plush blue longue chair in the VIP hospitality suite of Durabia Cove Jewelry, located in the mall, and asked her to wait for his return.

She had noticed the furtive glance in her direction from the stunning blonde attendant as she said, "This way Mr. Avery," and guided Dallas through a closed black metal door.

When he reappeared he seemed nervous, she had never seen him that way, so her interest was piqued. His over six-foot frame transformed as he lowered to one knee beside her, his right hand slid into his shirt pocket and he held her left hand with his, and said, "Will you take a chance on us, Alicia Mitchell, and marry me?"

With tears streaming down her cheeks, Alicia knew it was right. "Yes, my love. Yes," She said enthusiastically.

The thoughts of their age difference and her feeling that children were not in the cards faded with those words.

"I want everyone to know you are mine," he whispered, as they clung to each other.

"You're getting awfully possessive and jealous-like," she had responded jokingly, while extending her left hand and allowing him to slip the ring onto her finger.

"I've always been." He lowered his head and kissed the ringed hand.

"You know, Dallas," she placed her lips close to his right ear, "You have a problem with everyone that has a penis who looks at me sideways." Alicia stuck her elbow in his side and laughed.

Dallas threw his head back and roared with laughter, "And what if I do? Can you blame me?"

She looked up as cheers erupted, she hadn't been aware of the audience since she fastened her eyes on Dallas the minute he walked back into the room.

As her gaze scanned the faces, her eyes widened, and the smile broadened as she recognized Kamran, Luna, and the blond attendant. "What are you guys doing here?' she asked as she stood to greet them and accepted congratulations and hugs. They'd later returned to Kamran's residence where he hosted a lavish celebratory meal prepared by his staff.

She felt Dallas' breath against the soft curve of her neck and his lips and tongue sending chills and tingles all over her body. She tried to turn around, but his arm tightened, and he pulled her closer against him. He swept her dark silky hair over one shoulder and continued to rain kisses on her neck and upper back.

"Don't stop," she responded in a breathy whisper, then twisted around to face him, took his lips, and pulled him in and held on tight.

"Oh, baby." He moved her to an arm's length away and his eyes roamed her body, then lifted her nightgown and said, "You're bare down there."

"Sorry my love, I'll be right back," Alicia whispered and touched her lips against his then slowly pushed away.

"Are you gonna leave me hanging like that?' he asked with a smile, then hesitantly released her before adjusting his blue and gold elastic waist lounge pants while keeping his eyes focused on her every move.

Alicia slid off the bed, stood at the bedside looking down at him for a moment then sashayed towards the kitchen. As her right hand touched the golden doorknob and turned the lock, she heard a sweet melody and wheeled around, almost losing her balance.

"All of me, loves all of you. I love your curves and all your edges ..." Dallas bust out the John Legend tune at the top of his voice, arms opened wide and stretched towards the woman he loved more than anything in the world.

Alicia stopped in her tracks, with eyes wide and her face lit up in a smile. Without skipping a beat, she taunted, "First of all, don't quit your day job. Second ..." She then harmonized the rest, "All of me, loves all of you ..."

As she slowly sauntered towards him, her eyes lowered to the tent in the front of his pants and she felt a twinge of envy towards the material that covered it. Her gaze cruised back up past the V above the low pants waist, the six-pack and up to his pecs of steel or was it chromium? She rushed back into his arms. He grabbed, swung her around and gently landed her on the plush white carpet. One hand travelled downwards and cupped her buttocks while the other reached to her silky hair as his lips claimed her. As their bodies became entwined, she stood on tiptoes and thrusts her hips into him.

Two hearts singing as one in harmony. *For now.*

Dallas & Alicia's Story Continues in Open Door Marriage

`Three years later . . .`

Thanksgiving - Chicago, Illinois
November 22—7:23 p.m.

"You slept with my aunt?"

The words still didn't register, even though this had to be Tori's fifth time saying them. She glared at her fiancé, still desperately trying to come to terms with the information her mother had blasted to everyone at the packed Thanksgiving dinner table.

"Seriously? How is that even humanly possible when you didn't know the woman four hours ago?" Tori shouted.

"Tori, l-let me explain," Dallas stammered.

Twelve pairs of eyes were now focused on the not-quite-blissful couple standing at the bottom of the stairs just off from the dining room.

"But not here. Let's go somewhere and talk. It's not what you think."

"What did you do?" Tori snapped, glaring up at him. "Trip over the sheets, and your penis somehow landed in a woman nearly twice my age?"

The drumstick in Uncle Bill's hand paused in midair on its journey to his wide mouth. Cousin Tiny's fleshy hand flew to her overexposed bosom and came to rest somewhere above her heart. Even her father's frozen expression of alarm would have been Three Stooges comical if the situation weren't so tragic.

Aunt Yoli was the first to recover. "Did she just say what I think she said?"

In unison, everyone nodded.

"Girl, shut the front door and run out the back!"

A few bursts of nervous laughter sprang up around the table, but they were not nearly enough to chase away the unease that had flooded the room when Tori stepped into the house. She'd gone to drop off Aunt Rose's drunk self at home. Tori hadn't even been in the house good when her mother, Bernice, blurted out that she'd caught Alicia and Dallas together. Alone. In bed. In the nude. Tori had picked up from there and summed it up in one sweep. "You slept with my aunt ..."

"Nothing happened," Dallas said, his voice solid. "I didn't sleep with her."

"So, my mama's lying?" Tori asked.

Dallas shifted uneasily.

"Hell naw. I know what I saw," Bernice snapped. She had moved from the dining room table to the end of the staircase, right next to her daughter, poised as if she was ready to go to battle. "Both of you were in bed butt-ass naked." She jabbed a finger in her sister-in-law's direction. Alicia hadn't moved from her spot at the top of the staircase. Probably, because she knew what was best for her. "She was butt-naked. And he was nut-naked," Bernice yelled. "Wasn't an inch of space between them." She flickered a gaze at Dallas. "Look at him. You can tell he just got dressed."

Tori closed her eyes and took deep breaths to calm the emotions that warred within her.

"See, I told you Alicia wasn't worth a damn," Bernice crowed with savage satisfaction. "And looks like Mr. NBA ain't much better. You thought he was all that and a side order of fries."

Dallas Avery was the NBA's most valuable player, and a man most women would give their right and left ovary to call their own. But Most Eligible Bachelor or not, he had set Tori's bitch meter into overdrive. Even with his chiseled, handsome face, towering muscular frame, and million dollar bank accounts, he was now worth next to nothing in her eyes. Too bad her aching heart didn't get that memo.

Tori didn't know if she was more enraged or hurt that her mother had been all too willing to drive this stake through her own daughter's heart in order to publicly disgrace Alicia.

"We need to talk about this," Dallas repeated before adding, "in private."

Bernice wore a satisfied smirk as she glared openly up at Alicia, who just kept staring stoically at them from the second floor landing. "The angel of the family has fallen," Bernice said.

"Hey, Bernice," Bill taunted with a hearty chuckle. "Bet you won't say that when Alicia comes downstairs. You know she's gonna put a hurting on you."

"You mean put *another* hurting on her," Aunt Yoli added, doubling over with laughter.

Tori wanted to scream. Her life was unraveling in front of her, and her family was cracking jokes.

Instinctively, Bernice inched away from the staircase and back toward the dining room table. Her hands went up to the scar on her neck, probably remembering that a year ago on this very same holiday, Alicia had ended a vicious blow-for-blow fight with a knife at Bernice's throat. Almost gave the woman a "Sicilian Smile"—an ear-to-ear slice across the throat.

Dallas reached for Tori's hand. "It's not what it seems."

She snatched away, parted her lips to give him what was left of her mind, but Cousin Tiny chimed in first. "Alicia had every right to take Bernice to the floor last year for that foul mess she said. I would've pulled out my own can of whoop ass behind that one."

Tiny's husband, Thomas, nodded his watermelon-sized head.

The rest of the family finally sprang to life, also chiming in at once to defend Alicia, the one woman everyone could count on in a time of need, to lend an ear when it was called for and to dry a tear when no one else bothered to care. That she would do something as low as sleep with her niece's soon-to-be husband was unthinkable. So the family sidestepped that issue for as long as they could, finding it more comfortable to speak on the reason no one had expected Alicia home for Thanksgiving—especially since none of them had heard from her for an entire year.

Dallas maneuvered so he was in front of Tori. "Nothing. Happened."

"If Bernice had said that bull to me," Bill responded, still trying to tackle the last of the drumstick, "an ass whipping would've been the least of her problems." He beckoned toward the last slice of sweet potato pie at the other end of the table. "That has my name written all over it."

"Bernice is lying," Martha said. "Alicia's still got looks and all, but that young stud wouldn't pick her over Tori." She shot an appreciative glance toward Dallas, then leaned to her right and whispered loudly in Yoli's direction, "But, girl, he is finer than frog's hair."

Yoli gave him a lusty once-over. "I'd give him some my damn self. He's the type of man who can make a woman put a for sale sign on one thigh and an open for business sign on the other. Yes, Lawd."

Tori tried her best to tune out her family. She didn't have the stamina to deal with them right now. "How could you do this? You're my fiancé."

"You're Tori's fiancé?" Alicia finally spoke out. She eased down the stairs, looking first to Tori then to Dallas. Her panic-stricken expression gave Tori pause. Could her aunt really have not known?

Alicia turned back to her niece. "Oh, my, God, Tori. I had no idea. I'm so, so sorry." She didn't give Tori time to reply as she brushed past Dallas, slipped into the nearest pair of shoes—her brother's—and ran out of the front door, oblivious to the fact that she barely had on enough clothing to protect her from the chill in the room, let alone the sub-zero temps of a Chicago winter.

The whole crowd gasped in disbelief as Dallas grabbed his leather coat from the foyer closet. "She can't go out there with nothing on," he said as he stepped into his Timberlands. "I'll be right back."

Tori was ready to spit fire. "Are you kidding me?" she screamed as he quickly laced up his shoes, then darted toward the door. "You're going after my aunt? My aunt," she yelled, following him. "My heart is bleeding all over the carpet and you're going after *her*."

The front door slammed, and Tori stood frozen, unable to believe what happened in the last ten minutes. Bernice's voice snapped Tori out of her trance. "Girl, I taught you better than that," Bernice yelled, gesturing to the door. "You'd better go get your man."

Tori snatched up a coat and scarf and braced herself against the frigid gust of wind that slapped her as she left the house. She trekked across the snow and barely reached Dallas before he pulled off. Banging on the glass, she demanded, "Where the hell are you going?"

Dallas lowered the window. "She's out there unprotected. None of this is her fault."

"So now you're speaking up for her, too?" Tori screeched, pummeling him through the opening. "What kind of bullshit is that?"

Dallas flinched at her vicious tone and reached out to keep her hands from doing any more damage. "I'm going to say two things," he replied in that businesslike tone that had landed him several million-dollar endorsement deals. "I'm sorry that your mother lied to you, but nothing happened." His gaze swept the area, probably searching for the woman who was the center of the chaos. "And I'd be less of a man than you already think I am if I let that woman walk around in this weather without a coat."

Tori gave his words a moment's consideration. Causing a scene wouldn't stop him from doing what he felt he had to do, so she made a dash for the passenger side. "I'm coming with you."

They caught up with Alicia at the end of Harper Avenue, where she made a left and was now struggling up the path a block away from the main thoroughfare. She was shaking uncontrollably from the cold and from the sobs that wracked her body.

"Get in, Alicia," Dallas commanded, trailing the distraught woman as she stumbled along the icy sidewalk in shoes that were three sizes too big.

Alicia covered her mouth as though to keep in the words that threatened to spill out. She continued forward, wavering while trying to balance in the oversized loafers on snow that came up to her calves on unshoveled parts of the sidewalk.

"Don't make me get out of the car," Dallas said through his teeth.

Alicia ignored the threat, forcing the car to continue following her until she made it to a glass bus shelter on Stony Island Avenue. She swept the snow away from the steel bench, crawled on it, then tucked her legs up under her as though preparing to spend the night.

Dallas was out of the car and by her side in the time it took to blink. He whipped off his leather coat, placed it about Alicia's shoulders, then held out his hand to her. It took a moment for her to take it, but finally she stood. Together, they took two steps, then, she crumbled down onto the snow.

"Ouch," she shrieked. "My ankle."

It took Dallas only a moment to lift her into his arms, then navigate carefully over the slick pavement. He placed her gently, almost lovingly, in the back seat of his rented Benz. Using the sleeve of his shirt, he wiped her tears away.

Tori felt like she was having an out-of-body experience. The way Dallas looked at Alicia. The way he held her. It tore at Tori's gut. "Dallas, what's going on?" Tori asked once he was back in the driver's seat. "How the hell have you connected with her in such a way that you feel obligated to ease her pain and not mine?" The anger was still there, but Tori tried to push it aside, because right now, she needed clarity.

Dallas carefully pulled onto the street and aimed the car back in the direction of the place they'd just left. "We'll talk about this when we get back to the house."

"No," Alicia cried out, gripping the edge of the driver's seat and causing Dallas to punch the brakes. "I can't go back there. Not right now."

Dallas locked gazes with her in the rear view mirror. "Where do you want me to take you?"

"I don't know. Anywhere but there," she whispered, slumping back down in the seat. "Anywhere but home." Alicia's shoulders shook with an effort to hold herself together, and Dallas' expression softened.

The whole scenario made Tori's heart constrict as though someone had put a vise grip on the very thing that kept her alive.

She had only been gone for three hours. What the hell had happened between Dallas and her aunt?

"You risked your life for my grandson," Sheikh Aayan said, his voice echoing through the ornate throne room. "Ask for anything and I will see what can be done."

Ellena scanned the expectant faces of the throngs of people who had gathered for this unexpected audience with the ruler of Durabia. Most of their tunics and dishdashas differed from her casual attire of a simple white blouse and black slacks. "Thank you, but that isn't necessary. I did what anyone would do."

"Evidently, not everyone," he said, and his angry glare focused on the bodyguard, caregivers, and everyone who had stood by when Javed, the little royal, had swept past Ellena and landed on the moving conveyor belt.

All of them had frozen in place the moment Javed brushed against the rubber bounding strip and was sucked into the void. The video of Ellena dropping her tote bag, diving in after him, and cradling him in her arms as they were both tossed through the maze of steel and vinyl, all while being battered by suitcases and duffel bags alike, went viral.

Ellena had closed her eyes, bracing under each blow. Javed's laughter was a stark contrast to her pain. The cameras caught everything, including the tail end of the journey when Ellena tumbled out of the final drop onto another belt and finally into the metal cart that would carry the luggage onto the plane. Security finally found their legs and scrambled to make it to Ellena and the little boy before they sustained further injuries. Well, before she did. Her fleshy body was all the protection that Javed needed.

Javed Khan, a great grandson of the Royal Family, was completely unharmed. Ellena, on the day of arrival for a class reunion vacation, had to be rushed to the hospital. They kept her overnight. She sustained a few cuts and bruises that matched the dent in her ego when the entire world saw her tossed head over ass multiple times. And when the adrenaline wore off and the fear kicked in, the little royal refused to let her go. He even had to travel in the emergency transport with her because none of the guards or caregivers managed to force him to release his hold on Ellena.

Now she stood in a palace situated in the heart of a metropolis in the Middle East with a décor that was unrivaled by anything she'd ever seen. Gold—everything was layered with it—the walls, doors, accented by purples and reds that added a sultry warmth to all of the opulence of the furniture, paintings, and draperies covering massive windows.

"Well, to be honest, I haven't wanted much," she said with a nervous laugh. "And the only thing I don't have is a husband. But I'd love to have a place here in Durabia, where I can come and go as I please. If that is at all possible."

"Done," the Sheikh said, beckoning to the man who had visited the hospital twice to see about her condition. "Kamran, come."

"Wait. What?" She laughed and rested a hand on her ample bosom. "An apartment, really?"

"Your new husband," he answered with a grand gesture that would have made Vanna White proud. "This is my oldest son."

The man was drop-dead gorgeous. Olive complexion, dark hair, goatee neatly trimmed to perfection, and piercing brown eyes that missed nothing. He was more suited to a fashion runway than a palace. Truthfully, she wasn't sure if it was the tunics, neat beards, head coverings or what. Durabia seemed to have no shortage of handsome men. But the Sheikh's son was a masterpiece, exuding the kind of confidence that came with a man who was certain of his place in the world. His gaze swept across her face with a complexion slightly darker than his olive tone, then quickly covered the distance over her curves, then his lips lifted in a warm, appreciative smile that practically lit up his dark brown eyes and sent heat straight to places that had been dormant since the Queen of Sheba caused King Solomon to lose his entire mind.

Ellena shook her head, clearing her mind of all manner of wickedness that came after that wonderful assessment. "I think you misunderstood. I was joking about the husband part. The apartment, time share or whatever you call them here, that's all I really want."

"You will have both," the Sheikh commanded with a nod of finality no one would dare to question. "A husband and a place here. My son needs a wife and you mentioned you do not have a husband. Problem solved."

"But doesn't he have to give you heirs or something?" She instinctively brought her hands near her belly. "My eggs are old enough to be married and have children of their own by now."

First, a roar of laughter went up from him. A few moments later, it was mirrored by everyone standing around her. Yes, that line was funny, but the one thing she understood was the unfairness of the situation. At least for Kamran. And that was no laughing matter.

The Sheikh waved away that thought. "That will not be a concern. He is unable to give you or any woman children. And a woman of African descent will never sit on the Durabian throne. We are safe on that score."

A shadow of sadness flickered in Kamran's eyes and his skin flushed a shade darker. Ellena tried to read a deeper meaning into his father's words. She still came up with *unfair.* "So, you just throw him to a random woman because he can't give you an heir? He is *still* a man. He *still* has value," she insisted. "A brain, intelligence, and a purpose." She inhaled, trying to tamp down on her anger. "The apartment is fine, Sheikh. Thank you, but I will not be foisted on a man who has no say in the matter. That's downright cruel."

A gasp came from the core of people around them before silence descended in the room. Even Kamran flinched.

The Sheikh's face darkened with anger as he slowly came to his feet. "Are you refusing—"

"Give me nine days—"

All eyes focused on the handsome man, who left his father's side and moseyed toward her like some type of Arabian cowboy. All swagger, no gun necessary.

"Give me nine days," he repeated and moved across the expensive Persian carpet until he stood in front of her, towering over her near six-foot height by three inches of his own. "Nine days for me to show you Durabia, to answer any questions you may have. To let you explore the place, the people, the culture. Then you decide."

Ellena found it hard to catch her breath. The man was so virile she felt warm all the way to her follicles. "Nine days? I have to go home. I have a job back there. I used all of my vacation and two of my sick days for this trip."

"Your job?" he asked, frowning as though he couldn't fathom what the word meant.

"Yes. A job. Nine to five. Benefits. All of that. You know, what regular folks do to keep an address."

Kamran remained silent for a few moments as he peered at her. "How much do they pay you?"

She winced, then flickered a gaze to his right and felt the intensity of everyone's attention. "It doesn't matter."

"How much?" He beckoned for her to come nearer. "Whisper it to me."

Ellena hesitated a moment, then complied, moving so close she inhaled the intoxicating scent of sandalwood. She managed to whisper an answer, then inched back to put a little distance between them.

"For the rest of your life?" he asked, his tone and wide eyes reflecting the incredulity registered in his facial expression.

"Until I'm sixty-seven and retire," she replied, daunted by his tone. "But there's also health benefits and other factors that I can't put a number on."

Kamran blinked as though doing a set of mental calculations and coming up with what probably amounted to simple interest on his bank account. "Give me the particulars and I will wire the money into your account."

She parted her lips to protest but he held up a hand. "Saying yes to taking me as your husband is still your choice. With this, I am simply ensuring your peace of mind. And as a gift for your kindness, your selflessness in saving a child who was a stranger to you."

Ellena let out a long, slow breath, because staying here permanently, marrying him, would be a lost cause. She loved her job as a personal assistant at Vantage Point. Alejandro Reyes, a "Fixer" of everything from political and corporate espionage, to terrorist attacks, was the absolute best person to work for. And she loved the predictability of her life. Traveling overseas was the most adventurous event in her life. Still, curiosity won out over common sense and she said, "All right. Thank you."

"Now we go about the business of getting to know one another," he said, smiling as though her consent brought him much pleasure. Evidently, he wanted this to happen and the intensity of his gaze bore into her soul. "So that you can make an informed decision, yes?"

She glanced over his shoulder, taking in some of the envious looks a few of the women tried to hide. "Why are you doing this?" she asked him. "Why are you allowing them to serve you up to some foreign woman as if you do not have value?"

"Because I recognize this is God's will," he answered. "And who am I to leave a precious gift unwrapped?"

Her eyebrows drew in, as she tried to decipher the hidden meaning behind his words. The man had a peaceful, confident air but also a playful vibe about him.

"Yes, that was a double entendre." His smile widened and she could swear the heavens opened up and smiled with him.

Good Lord, I'm in trouble.

Things That Keep Me Up At Night

Open secrets are seldom spoken about. The way the mind works is curious. Some memories are dear to us and we want to hold on to them forever, while erasing others. However, to share my life journey I must scan my brain for the good and bad. The incidents or memories I want to forget are the ones on perpetual rewind, and some that need to be recalled have been permanently deleted. I often pray that the painful recollections will vanish, like some people, from my life. However, they seem to be glued closer than family.

I grew up in a large extended family in the parish of Clarendon, Jamaica but wasn't born there. However, life prior to that is a complete blur. My maternal grandparents had lived in England for many years and retired to Jamaica. The five-bedroom house was always filled with people, family, and friends.

On special occasions, we congregated at my grandparents' house, which was the venue for all major happenings.

One such event occurred in the Summer of 1973. One female family member was there for a home birth. The women were excited and busy with the preparations for the baby. While everybody rushed around, I sat on the living room sofa reading a book. I had started reading at an early age and always carried a book in hand.

The man seated beside me was there for the birth, and not directly involved in the process. In those days, men weren't encouraged to take part in the birthing, so he was reading the newspaper, which he spread across my legs and his.

The back of the sofa was against the bedroom wall where the birthing team was occupied. The woman in labor was moaning and groaning in obvious distress. One of the doors leading in and out of that bedroom was to the right of where we sat, and someone could have appeared at any minute.

Since it was their first child, I expected him to show some compassion for her discomfort. He didn't give any indication that he heard his wife, or that he was aware of what had been happening so close to where we were situated.

This pervert was bold. I had not thought about it then, but it was obviously not his first rodeo. He had to have done this before, without any repercussions.

Without saying a word, he shifted closer as his hand crept up the inside of my legs underneath the paper. I was paralyzed with shock and fear as he attempted to put his fingers in my vagina. The only thing I had the strength to do was clamp my legs shut. However, he kept trying to force his hand between my thighs.

I would not relent and could not stand.

His fumbling seemed to have gone on for hours, although I'm sure it was only a few minutes. When he realized I wasn't moving or opening my thighs, he laughed, pulled away, and continued reading the paper as if nothing out of the ordinary had happened.

I was eleven years old.

Neither of us moved for a while. For the rest of that day and the following weeks the feeling of disgust remained with me. Although I avoided being near him, I don't believe anyone noticed.

Back then, child sexual abuse and domestic violence were rampant in my community. This one man later molested multiple young girls in the family and, from reports, in the district as well. Although the adults knew, nothing was ever done. Open secrets were seldom or not spoken about at all. Would they have acted if I had said anything? I didn't believe anyone would've had the courage to confront him. Not that I thought they were afraid of him, but because my family wasn't known to be confrontational.

Could I have saved some of the later victims if I had told someone about what he did?

The thought still hurts to this day. I never told anyone because I didn't want to make things bad for my family, especially my aunt and her newborn. If I spoke up, I believed it would've brought shame and disgrace on the family. Only a few people have heard this story and not in detail. I was in my forties before I finally mentioned it to my aunt,

Lyn. I recalled how surprised she had been. However, she didn't confirm what I had learned from another family member, that she too, had been a victim of that same individual. At the time it was mentioned, I was an adult and we were discussing the pedophile in the family and his many known and suspected victims.

To my knowledge, to this day, he has never been confronted. Everyone in the family and majority of the community had knowledge of this.

It's shameful and tragic that the "village" that provided clothing, food and shelter, also would not step forward to protect a child from sexual abuse. Why is that? When I was in my early twenties, I struck up a conversation with a forty-something-year-old woman in the community about the subject. She was unable to think of an answer to my question. However, she relayed a story that shocked me these many years later.

She said, "I know somebody who that happened to."

"Really" I said, "Who?"

"My neighbor, Michelle's six-year-old daughter. Every time she lef for work," she replied in Jamaican Patois, "her boyfriend molest de child."

With eyes and mouth opened wide, I asked, "How do you know that for sure?"

She responded, "They would be alone inside the house for a while, and when she came outside, she can barely walk and always eating a bag of chips."

My tone increased by a few decibels, "Did you tell her mother?"

"No! It's none of my business."

"That is the same damn thing we were just talking about," I yelled "Nobody gives a rat's ass about the children."

She lowered her head.

"What if it were your daughter?" I continued.

"I would kill him if I found out," she said, now angry.

"How would you find out if everybody shares your opinion?" I scolded.

The conversation ended abruptly and we exchanged goodbyes. The incident was never mentioned again.

By the time I heard the story, the mother and child had relocated and I haven't heard of or seen them since. Over the years, I thought of her and wondered about the woman she has grown into.

In February of 2021, I was a guest on The Stay-At-Home Nurse podcast, where I was interviewed on my role as a Sexual Assault Nurse Examiner. During the episode I spoke publicly, for the first time, about being a victim of childhood sexual abuse.

After I shared the broadcast, family and friends, while offering congratulations on my successes, also expressed shock and sadness about the abuse. Some came forward and shared their experiences with sexual trauma.

One victim was six years old when she was first abused.

As she recounted her experience, she stated that the abuse began with the man's fingers and advanced to penile penetration.

Dear God, I cringe to imagine the torture she endured at the hands of the villain.

As a result of my revelation, I learned, there were more victims and sexual perverts, in my family than I could have ever imagined.

About *Things That Keep Me Up At Night*

If you've ever wondered whether faith and determination are a recipe for success, " Things That Keep Me Up at Night" answers that question.

Marie takes you through her journey from adversity to triumph in this compelling memoir. From sexual assault at the age of eleven, through to becoming a successful Registered Nurse, Marie charts her path through the hills and valleys on the way to success.

She pays tribute to the people who inspired, encouraged, and supported her through various stages of her journey.

Her work as an advocate for victims of sexual assault and rape, domestic violence, and homelessness will encourage those who have been through similar experiences and need their hope restored.

About Marie McKenzie

Marie McKenzie is a #1 Amazon Bestselling author of her first book, a memoir, "Things That Keep Me Up at Night," which was released in June of 2021. She is an accomplished Registered Nurse, educator, community volunteer, victims' advocate, and trained Sexual Assault Nurse Examiner. Born in Jamaica, Marie migrated to the United States of America in 1989, and currently resides in Orlando, FL, with her husband George.

She is a member of the NK Tribe Called Success, which mentors and supports aspiring authors and provides a home for experienced authors to advance their craft and business acumen.

90 Days of Pleasure is her first fiction work which she co-authored with *USA TODAY* Bestselling Author, Naleighna Kai.

Website: www.marielmckenzie.com

Sociatap: https://Sociatap.com/MarieL

About Naleighna Kai

Naleighna Kai is the *USA TODAY, Essence®*, and national bestselling and award-winning author of several women's fiction, contemporary fiction, Christian fiction, romance, erotica, and science fiction novels that plumb the depth of unique relationships and women's issues. She is also a contributor to a *New York Times* bestseller, one of AALBC's 100 Top Authors, a member of the CVS Hall of Fame, a Mercedes Benz Mentor Award Nominee, and the recipient of the E. Lynn Harris Author of Distinction award.

She continues to "pay it forward" by organizing the annual Cavalcade of Authors which gives readers intimate access to the most accomplished writing talent today. She also established and heads up the NK Tribe Called Success, which offers aspiring and established authors assistance with ghostwriting, developmental editing, publishing, marketing, and other services to jump-start or enhance their writing careers.

https://bit.ly/NaleighnaKai

10 Days of Pleasure

Some relationships are made in the storm. Real love survives them. Basketball star Dallas Avery has the world in the palm of his hand and a lifetime of happiness or despair within his grasp. For accomplished businesswoman, Alicia Mitchell, love is a double-edged sword wrought with happiness and pain. Business calls the soulmates to Scotland but a new, more treacherous storm is brewing back home. Can their love weather this latest test, or will a crueler fate prevail?

20 Days of Pleasure

NBA star Dallas Avery has one intention when he visits the most romantic city in the world—win Alicia Mitchell by any means necessary. They relish their time as a couple—free to explore their magnetic connection in Paris and savor the array of pleasures they discover as soul mates.

But family, friends, the media, and society at large, have various opinions about their complicated relationship. Will Dallas and Alicia find a way to stay together, or will the many factors working against them shatter their once-in-a-lifetime romance?

30 Days of Pleasure

Every end is supposed to be a beginning. After the death of her husband, Alicia Mitchell set herself up financially to embrace freedom and see the world. Then she met a detour. Until NBA basketball star Dallas Avery wrapped his arms around her, Alicia didn't know what it felt like to be cherished. Now he's drawing her focus and shifting her priorities. And Alicia doesn't mind. However, there's a shadow creeping from the edges of her dating history.

Taric Hasan, a man she considered dating until she experienced his dark side, has emerged. Although she once managed to escape him, Taric isn't done with her. He's intent on ending their relationship on his terms … with her death.

40 Days of Pleasure

The NBA's sexy and most valuable player Dallas Avery meets the beautiful Alicia Mitchell, who has one thing on her mind: leaving. Their attraction is intense, but the timing is off. Dallas is determined to convince Alicia to give their May-December relationship a chance, but when their romantic trip to the Caribbean gets derailed by them being embroiled in a local family's deadly drama, romance gets put on the back burner.

50 Days of Pleasure

When an obsessive fan threatens to derail Basketball Superstar Dallas Avery's relationship with the alluring and independent Alicia Mitchell, a trip to Canada comes at the opportune time. The historic sites and chilly landscapes help to stir the growing connection between the couple.

Then a distressed infant is thrust into their care. The teenage mother and her baby are in danger and only trust Dallas and Alicia to help. With the local mob in pursuit and Dallas and Alicia unable to depend on the police, they must flee the country using a historic mode of escape.

60 Days of Pleasure

Determined to give Alicia Mitchell the love that she longs for, NBA-star Dallas Avery whisks her away on exciting adventures around the world.

Dallas let his heart dictate their journey to Seattle and allows the Emerald City to work its magic on Alicia. Until civil unrest involving the indigenous people collides with a dirty politician's plans to use city funds to cover personal debts. A chance meeting with Yuma, a tribal chief's son, creates an opportunity for Dallas to make a difference for those whose voices have been silenced. When an altercation with the police develops after Dallas and Alicia assist a homeless woman, Yuma's tribe is forced to shift gears and protect the couple.

Can Dallas keep the love of his life safe, and will the civil unrest drive a permanent wedge between them?

70 Days of Pleasure

Dallas Avery and Alicia Mitchell are off to Nashville, Tennessee for business and pleasure. Unfortunately, the past returns to haunt the basketball superstar and puts both in imminent danger.

Conway Ackerman has spent the last five years in prison, charged with aggravated stalking of the athlete early in his career. A bitter man with a sordid past, and a psychotic personality, Ackerman has recently been let out of prison and has set a course that will exact the perfect revenge.

While Dallas is aware of the convict's release, he keeps Alicia in the dark. The stage is set for a myriad of adventures, which will extend to the iconic Beale Street in Memphis, but danger is in the midst. A race against time ensues as the couple is tracked from place to place. Will they survive or meet their demise at the hands of a man whose mental state is deadly?

80 Days of Pleasure

From a romantic picnic in the Southwest to jet-setting around the globe to exotic destinations, Dallas Avery lays the foundation for a long-lasting relationship with Alicia Mitchell, brick by brick, beginning with these five words, "Just one more day, baby."

While traveling the romantic countryside from Munich, Germany to Schloss Neuschwanstein, a case of mistaken identity threatens their freedom and possibly their lives. Dallas has faced numerous threats, but nothing could have prepared him for this experience. A desire to make Alicia's childhood dream come true has evolved into an incredible nightmare.

Dallas and Alicia struggle to learn the new rules of engagement they have been forced to play by. One thing is certain, the NBA player is determined they will not be on the losing end.

90 Days of Pleasure

Alicia Mitchell, is and was, the only woman Dallas Avery has ever loved. He strives to soothe her fears about their age difference, the unresolved issues of her past, and is determined to make her his forever.

An impromptu trip to Durabia brings more danger to their relationship. Crown Prince Amir sets his sights on Alicia and puts a diabolical plan in motion for her to be secretly brought into the palace where he can have her all to himself. None of them could fathom that a third party would intervene, and plunge Dallas and Alicia in the middle of a brotherly war.

USA TODAY Bestselling Author, Naleighna Kai, tells the dynamic love triangle of a chance encounter that lands wealthy NBA star, Dallas Avery, back in the arms of Alicia, the woman of his dreams. A woman he hasn't seen in years. A woman he soon discovers is his fiancée's long-lost aunt!

But Tori, isn't ready to give up all that she's worked for in their relationship, so she makes him a shocking offer—go through with the wedding and she'll still allow him to be with the one woman he now can't seem to do without. Dallas will get a family, something her aunt can't give him and Tori will have the lifestyle she clamors. And Alicia will embrace the love she's longed for all her life and that had already been in her reach before she disappeared. Everyone will get a little of what they want. . . and maybe a whole lot of what they don't.

The details of the trio's love life play out in the tabloids and on talk shows, making Dallas the center of an NBA scandal. Eventually, the doors slam shut on this open marriage in the making and Dallas is forced to make a choice to end the chaos.